Feast: A Gitksan Story

by

Roy W. Russell

Dedication

This is dedicated to both of my *Ye'eh's* Burt and Gordon, to my *Na'ah* Mary, my *Geech* Susan, my godmother Katie, and to my parents Gwen (*Ts'eegim Hanak*) and Don (Chief *Luux Hon*). Thank you for supporting me all these years, providing inspiration and love in everything I've done.

I thank my wife Lia for her feedback on this project, for her questions about our culture, and ensuring I best explained the concepts in this book to those unfamiliar with the Gitksan Feast system.

The art pieces featured on the cover were made by Katie Ludwig, *Galsimgiget*, a talented artist and dedicated preserver of Gitksan Culture, who created the Grouse Clan vest and the Gitksan carved mask.

As a member of the Grouse, I recognize our Chief Vernon Milton, *Xsgogimlaxha*, the proud leader of my House Clan in Gitsegukla. I would also like to take this opportunity to thank Ray Jones, *Niis Noolth*, for the mentoring and guidance he offered in my youth.

I thank my elders for answering my questions about how things are done in the Feast hall, why things are done in a certain way when our people grieve, and helping translate the words of my people.

Contents

Coming Home

Gasping, out of breath, he sits up in the dorm room listening to the wind blowing rain against the window, little tapping noises he finds calming. Toronto is always windy and rainy in the winter compared to the little Gitksan village he grew up in, Gitsegukla. Walt learned last year it was fruitless walking the metro streets with an umbrella. He stifled a defeated laugh when the wind took it from his hand, nearly hitting an older businessman on the sidewalk. Now sitting up in his bed, he regrets not sleeping on his side. He feels the burning in his chest as he coughs, trying to get as much air as he can into his lungs again. Today he got to sleep in, no classes until later in the afternoon. Listening for noises, the common room television isn't on, and the other roommates are at their arts or engineering classes. Walt gets up to enjoy breakfast in peace and take a nice long hot shower without interruption. He spends the next few hours enjoying the mundane: lying in bed listening to the radio, getting up to surf on the internet, and snacking on his favorite cheese-flavored chips. In that moment he forgets the worries, the shame, and a nasty spiral of depression that has been consuming him for the past couple of weeks. Walt thought he was doing well; he studied hard with Sam in their computer science classes and worked on his programming techniques, but it wasn't good enough. Walt sits quietly thinking about home. It is an entire day's flight from Toronto to Vancouver. A brief wait before connecting from Vancouver to Smithers. An hour-and-a-half drive from Smithers to the little village under the mountain. Everyone he ever knew and loved was back there hoping he would do his best in the big city, and taking advantage of the opportunity given to him. He liked to think he was a smart person who did well with the advanced math classes and computer programming, and now he wonders what brought him to this point?

The depression started two weeks ago. Walt is sitting at his desk trying to decipher the books he bought, text books he will get pennies for when selling them back at the end of the school year, the assigned homework feels like it is in a different language. Walt feels lost and out of place in Toronto. The night before he cried to himself quietly, not to alarm his friends, staring at the sleeping pills on top of his desk. *Take the pills, play some music, turn off the light, and go to sleep.* He planned it out in his head. The note was sitting there in the desk drawer addressed to his family. Nothing grand or elaborate, just a letter saying, "I'm sorry." Staring at the pills now, hearing himself breathe through his nose, wondering is this the day? He had always had a good outlook on life and enjoyed the company of his friends, and spending time with his favorite people at home. One morning, a funk settled in. Walt wants to go back home and regroup. He decides to not go to class in the afternoon. Maybe he should schedule a meeting with the academic advisor and find out his options. Can he salvage the situation and switch majors or transfer to a school back in British Columbia? Instead of crawling under the covers again he gets up, grabs the pill bottle, and flushes them down the toilet. "No, it will not be like this," he thinks to himself, "I will live."

After that he naps, dreaming of home once more. Of eating good Chinese food with his family in Terrace, or a bowl of salt fish and potatoes at his grandmothers, those are his favorite dreams. He likes being in Toronto with his new friends. His next-door roommate, James, is fun. James' girlfriend, Talia, is an all right girl in her odd Russian-raised ways. Sam went home to Quebec a week ago on family business, so an email will have to do for now.

Someone is knocking on the door. Nobody is home from class yet to answer. The rain has stopped, but you can still hear the swooshing sound of car tires disrupting the wet pavement on the street. The sound reminds him of trying to make the muddiest splash in the puddle in front of his parent's house eleven or twelve years earlier. The knocking at the door continues, sounding more urgent. Walt gets up from the nap, leaving his glasses on the desk. He's not that blind, he only needs them to see the white board at class lectures. It's nearly 8pm, and it's dark out now. Walt wonders where his roommates are right now. Maybe there's free pizza at the movie showing across the street. Walt is now annoyed with the knocking at the door, "Okay, I'm coming," he says walking to answer the door. "What the hell are you doing here, am I dreaming?" Walt opened the door, bleary eyed, and sees her standing there. She should be studying economics in Prince George. Walt sees his favorite cousin in the whole world, Angie.

Angie hugs Walt and looks him over to see if he's okay.

Walt realizes then what he had done—he hit send. Angie received the suicide note detailing the depression and booked a flight here in a flash. Her brown hair looks shorter than how it had been in September, no more curls. Walt thinks and smiles, "Cousin, you're the whitest-looking Indian I know."

The two sit on the red couch talking about the depression. Walt tries assuring Angie that he's okay, even showing her the empty pill bottle. That Walt decided he wants to live, and the suicide option isn't on the table anymore. Even with his explanation, Angie tells Walt it's time to go, time to leave this place and come home. She goes into Walt's bedroom and digs around, packing the suitcase, a graduation gift given by his godmother. Angie says, "I'm doing this for your parents, they were worried." Walt considers protesting, but this is how the family works. No secrets. Suicides happened back in Gitsegukla, not as rampant as the ones seen in Quebec or the Prairies, but enough to take even the threat seriously. "Nothing is wrong. Nobody is mad. We love you and just want for you to be happy," Angie says, zipping up the suitcase and handing Walt the laptop bag. Angie grabs the glasses off the desk and sits looking around at the bare college dorm room, "Figured you might have put up posters or something. It's just class schedules and a picture of us from the summer." The dorm manual had said it was against the rules to hang things up with pins. He hadn't yet gone to the college supply store to pick up that wall-friendly putty. Walt takes a last look at the empty dorm room and follows Angie, leaving the room behind.

The cab ride to the airport doesn't feel that long. The

two check in, making their way to the gate for a few hours of waiting before they catch the red-eye back to the West Coast. "I didn't mean to send that email. I don't mean what I wrote in it, not anymore at least." Walt tells Angie as he thinks of his now dark dorm room on St. George Street. Walt took a last stab at talking his way out of this situation, to get back on campus and maybe watch a classic movie with his fellow film nerds. Angie starts reading a book while Walt plays with his phone. Angie's mind can't be changed, the tickets are bought, and soon they'll board the plane. Walt eats a turkey sandwich for supper. Even though Angie was the one who came all this way to pick him up, it's Walt who stares at Angie wondering what's wrong. Did something happen between her and his best friend Doug? He tries to prod, but she isn't saying much, though she gladly accepts half of the sandwich he offered.

Not long after, they've finally boarded the plane. Walt sits next to the aisle, but can't find a comfy position to sleep and speed up the cross-country flight. Angie looks completely exhausted. There's a weight in her she's trying to carry, a loss in the glimmer of her eyes that troubles him. Did something happen between her and Doug? After the plane takes off Angie falls asleep, leaning against the plastic interior wall of the airplane. Walt looks around for the flight attendant to ask for a mini blanket. An Asian lady is sitting next to him on the other aisle and smiling at him. He smiles back, and then she starts speaking her native language leaving him confused. Walt wonders if he, a First Nations person, looks that Asian? It's not the first time that's happened since arriving in Toronto. He had gotten into the habit of telling people he's Native

American. The lady understands and puts headphones on and tries to go to sleep. The flight attendant makes his way to Walt, and he asks for two blankets for the Asian lady and Angie. Walt doesn't need a blanket—he knew going back to the frozen north he'd need a winter jacket and uses that instead. He still can't fall asleep, restless, thinking about his unexpected and unplanned homecoming. In the seat in front of him he sees the little face looking back at him, a blank stare, sucking on a pacifier. The mother quietly stealing a brief nap on the flight west. Walt smiles at the baby, and he smiles back, playing with the mother's long red hair in its tiny fingers. The baby has curly, dark brown hair, and bright blue eyes. The baby reaches through the gap between the seats, so Walt touches his little hand. It reminds him of the first time he held his sister Stephanie's little girl Denise. The baby turns his head resting on his mother's shoulder and goes to sleep. Walt decides to do the same, closing his eyes hoping he, too, can drift off to sleep.

Morning has already come to cloudy Vancouver as the plane lands. Walt and Angie try looking out the window, but can't see any of the beautiful mountains or buildings on the approach. With an hour to kill the two race to the fast food restaurant for egg sandwiches and coffee. Walt ventures into the strip mall section of the airport and finds a hockey jersey for Denise, who just turned three years old. Walt looks forward to seeing his little niece again and maybe taking her out sliding on the hills of Gitsegukla. Angie looks over the jersey, assuring him it will fit—she has also been buying her little cousin new clothes from the campus apparel store in Prince

George. The flight is much bumpier to Smithers and Angie holds on to the armrest of her seat. Walt laughs, assuring himself they're just too young to die. The jarring dips on the plane remind him of the old highway that leads from Prince Rupert to Cassiar. Walt's parents used to work the summer fishing and canning salmon in Cassiar—everyone from Gitsegukla worked on the coast. The road was narrow; it had a lot of hills, and if you drove on that road fast you would get butterflies in your stomach. That road made Walt's sister sick every time they'd go out there. Walt's dad, Gilbert, had to drive slower when she was in the car with them, but when she wasn't he would floor it for his son. His thoughts now turn to "The Bear". He died several years ago out on the coast, fishing for food and suffering a heart attack.

Coming home brings back memories of many people who won't be there to greet him when he arrives. Walt thinks of his grandfather and the epic trips they'd take up the mountain, hunting for goat, moose, or ground hogs. His grandfather had a large family comprised of seven sons and seven daughters. All of them, including the in-laws and grandchildren, walked a twisty, windy road up into the wild every fall. At the end of August, they went to gather food supplies for the coming winter. On one of those trips "The Bear" came with them. Halfway up the mountain the train of people needed to cross a long creek. To Walt, when he was six or seven, that creek looked like Niagara Falls. His grandfather had cut down trees to serve as a makeshift bridge to cross the rapid waters. Walt was scared of being swept away by the river and into the ocean. Then "The Bear" came along and asked Walt if he wanted to drive a truck. Walt didn't know what he was talking about, confused at the offer. "The Bear" bent down on his knees and told him to climb on his shoulders. He told Walt, "I'm your truck, and you drive me where you have to go." The two of them crossed that little creek with no problems. It saddens him every day his childhood hero isn't around anymore. Walt looks at Angie as she stares out the window at the snow-covered mountains. "The Little Bear", as she brings him back home safe to where he needs to be.

During the trip, Walt stresses about what he will say to people when he appears home. How much had Angie told them before she left school to pick him up? Walt had always been anxious in group settings or talking with people. Talia studied psychology and labeled him as having Asperger's. Walt didn't know if he agreed with that diagnosis, since talking about fake things is a waste of time. He might just be shy after years of being teased about girls by aunts and uncles, leaving him prone to avoiding people. Walt is glad when the plane lands and they're greeted solely by his sister Stephanie. She looks at her brother intensely. "I don't want to talk about it, not right now, not here," he says as he waits for the luggage. Soon they'll be in the car driving west, back to the little village by the mountain.

The snow has changed the landscape, and the wide open fields outside Smithers look like great places to race around in snowmobiles. Stephanie spends the first part of the ride talking about how Denise had graduated from crawling to walking on her own. Walt's father just installed a child gate so she won't go falling down the stairs. Walt shows Stephanie the hockey jersey, and she assures him the size is right, for now, until she grows out of it. Angie puts on the radio, and the three of them listen to the news. Walt, bored in the backseat, tugs at Angie's seatbelt, bugging her and laughing about it. When they arrive in Hazelton he looks at the now empty store fronts that used to line the highway. The economy isn't doing so well after the nearby forestry mills shut down. Walt looks at the clock on the dashboard; in twenty minutes he will be home. The whole trip has been a blur to him. Just yesterday he was in windy Toronto locked in his room staring out at traffic and the scurrying people four stories below on the sidewalks. Today, he sees the road leading into his village of Gitsegukla—they don't call it a reserve—home to the "People of the Mountain." The unpaved roads of his village have been sanded so people don't fall and cars don't crash into the ditches. Walt notes his grandmother's house when they drive past it. He plans to see her later on today, but for now they drive up the hill past the log house and pull into his parent's driveway. He looks around at just how quiet things are on his street. The kids are still in school up the hill learning English and Math. Most people who aren't at work are home watching daytime soaps or game shows. The gas station across from his parents' place is open—he'll pick up iced tea and chips later. The three of them walk inside the house, making their way up the stairs. Walt's parents hug him so hard when they get up the stairs. They ask if he's okay, if he's all right. He tells them he wasn't, that he wished things had worked out, and they reassure him things will get better. The anxiety and dread isn't there in his stomach anymore.

Walt takes his stuff to his bedroom, and he looks up at the carved wooden plaque signifying his stop. Everything is where he left it a few months ago. Graduation pictures of him, Angie, and his best friend, Doug, hang on the wall. His old computer sits in the corner on a desk with other family pictures. Walt sits on the bed, resting. Angie comes into the room and joins him. "Everything is here now, and you are home, Walt." Walt has been so worried and anxious about coming back he wondered about the sensation in his forehead. A tiny spot inches above his nose that has a mild tingling sensation. Like muscles getting sore after chopping firewood or hauling fish over his shoulder from the river. Has he been frowning this whole time? Walt asks for Angie's phone, and he takes a picture of himself. He looks at it and sees nothing. No weird expression visible or frown, just him. He lets out a small laugh as he gives the phone back to Angie. She looks at the photo, saves the picture, and puts the phone back in her pocket. Angie blurts out, "Oh yeah, this. This is yours." She takes out the glasses from her inside coat pocket and leaves them on the desk. She tells Walt she's going down to her mom's place and will try get back on their time zone. Walt hugs her and thanks her for bringing him back to Gitsegukla. Dead tired from the flights he takes a nap, laying on his bed, which was so much softer than his dorm bed. He can smell the cooking food his mom is making on the stove. He drifts off to sleep, exhausted from his long trip home. Out there, someone in Toronto is laying on their bed, listening to the rain being blown against the window. Walt can't believe it, as he fades off into sleep—he is home now and things feel better.

"What the hell are you doing here?" she yells, laughing as Walt enters the doorway of the tiny trailer next to the gas station pump. Running out from behind the counter she hugs him before he can answer. Michelle goes back to her seat behind the counter, and Walt looks over the store, picking up chips and pop. Michelle, another fellow graduate from high school, is Angie's best friend. Walt tells Michelle she's home now too. He doesn't know what to say to her original question. Instead, he grabs the headphones on the counter and listens to the music playing. "Life changed, listening to that has fixed your world and we can be a couple now, except I didn't spend my time calling you a retard and giggling obnoxiously. I saw that movie too. It was just on last month on the satellite television," Michelle says as she grabs her earphones back. She tries calling Angie on the phone, but there is no answer. Walt proceeds to exit, and Michelle makes him promise they'll properly catch up and that he'll say more than just a few words. Maybe he does have Asperger's, he thinks to himself as he walks down to his grandparents' place.

Grandmother's, actually. His grandfather died several years ago, so it's just her now. Walt's grandmother isn't alone, though. Her daughters and sons always stop by to visit, to share lunch or dinner, to watch hockey, or take her out to bingo. Walt's grandmother made a special dinner when she learned he was coming back. He sits at the table with two uncles and an aunt. They are all enjoying a hot plate of mashed potatoes mixed with chunks of salt fish, covered with Oolichan grease. The plate is called *Hashbadinner*. It is so much better than the tuna-based meals his roommates cooked back in Toronto. The uncles ask questions about hockey, if Walt had been able to catch any games while out there in the city. No, he had focused on school. Everyone moves to the couches to enjoy the 7pm game shows, yelling answers and keeping score of who was right the most. Walt can hear an uncle downstairs chopping wood for the fire. Walt listens to his aunt help her son with homework at the kitchen table. Cousin Eric is in a rush to get done so he can go sledding or have snowball fights with friends. Walt looks at the clock an hour and a half later and heads back home. His grandmother gives him large bowls of *Hashbadinner* for his mom, sister, and father in case they want some too. It's a quiet walk up the road for him, though Walt almost slips and falls once. When he gets home he discovers Angie and her mom playing with Denise. Putting the bowls of food on the table for people to discover when hungry, Walt tells Angie that Michelle is still at work across the street. She leaves to catch up with her friend. Angie's mom, who serves on the school board, tells Walt that things will be okay. It's not a big deal to change schools or switch majors, as long as he is happy and where he needs to be. Soon after, Angie's mom goes back to her house in the lower part of the village that is closest to the river.

Walt goes downstairs not long after checking the stove, which is full with slow-burning wood that will last the night. Peeking into the recreation room he sees the pool table and begins rolling the cue ball back and forth, letting it bounce against the sides. Stephanie comes downstairs, and the two sit on the couch. She asks if everything is okay. He recounts feeling hopeless, being so far away from home, isolated, and not knowing what to do some days. Walt kept up appearances with friends and roommates, but he wasn't well. He had left a brief note for friends telling them where he went and not to worry, relieved his sudden return home isn't terrible or embarrassing. Denise can be heard crying upstairs. Stephanie, being the big sister and now a mother, tells him if he ever needs to talk her *Mooxws* (ears) are open.

Walt sits at his desk playing computer pinball trying to beat the scores set by Angie. His father interrupts the gaming session to tell him that there's someone at the front door waiting. Downstairs, Michelle is geared up in a winter coat and thick snow pants, she says, "Come, let's go for a ride!" Walt hunts around looking for winter pants, coat, gloves, and a toque. The two stand outside staring at the snowmobile, silently figuring out who's going to drive. Michelle lets him go first. The two speed out of the driveway and up the hill toward the elementary school. They do a quick lap around the school, but avoid the field where the soccer teams play in the summer. Walt sees a mound of snow to launch off, and Michelle yells out "Woooo" while in mid-air. Then they head up an abandoned logging road called "The Y." This little road is where Walt's grandfather used to take him hunting for rabbits or trapping for furs when he was younger. When the two get to the top where the road splits, hence the name "The Y", Michelle wants to drive the snowmobile. "We can go faster, hold on tight," she says as they speed off into the darkness on a long stretch of road. Walt holds on so he doesn't fall off, cheeks freezing. Soon they turn around and go racing back into the village, and Michelle tries to hit the same jump.

Walt flies off the snowmobile landing face first into the snow, pushing himself up to her laughing, but she apologizes. Michelle had asked Angie if she had wanted to go, but she refused. He gets back on the snowmobile and Michelle drops him off at his house, then races off down the road to the lower part of the village. Behind Walt someone approaches and he hears the familiar voice.

"Hello friend." Walt looks around and sees Peter, who is on his way up to the gym to work setting up tables and chairs. The two briefly catch up, talking hockey.

Walt goes into his house, shaking off the snow from his winter clothes, hanging them up to dry next to the stove. He sees his mom standing at the top of the stairs, waiting in line to use the bathroom. The two can hear Michelle zoom by on her snowmobile.

Walt's mom utters, "Crazy girl, cops are going to get her if she isn't careful out there."

Nope, they've never caught her and never will, he thinks in response.

He sits with his dad, and the two quietly watch the news. Nothing major going on other than car accidents, protests about government spending, and hockey highlights. Walt decides to go to sleep, and Gilbert hugs him saying it's good to have him back again, "Good night, Walt." The house is now roasting. He opens the bedroom window just a little to let cool air drift over him. He lays staring out the window. No more worries, no more sadness, and he falls asleep to good dreams.

It was a hot summer day, the last day of August.

A soft and soothing voice asks, "Are you ready now?"

Walt turns around to see him, "The Bear"! He smiles and gives him a giant hug. Walt realizes this is a dream, and it makes him sad. He recognizes that they are outside the village on the logging road. A spot where family would park the trucks before making the long hike up the mountain. Walt wonders where they are going. "The Bear" smiles and points behind him, "With your *Ye'eh* to the mountain." As if his smile couldn't get bigger, when he thinks he couldn't be happier, Walt sees his grandfather holding a long walking stick. He runs to hug him; it's been so long since he's seen him.

"We're going up the mountain? What about everyone else?" Walt asks the two.

"The Bear" answers, "They'll catch up with us."

Excited, he wants to wake up from this dream to share it with everyone. It's so rare to have dreams about those who died. It's a gift to see their faces in your sleep. The three of them put on their backpacks, each with a walking stick, and step onto the familiar trail up the mountain. Just like they used to do in the olden days.

Seven Sirens

Today is a different day. A quiet morning in this little reserve, which is always quiet, because nothing happens. The clouds through the windows are dark and hint at another snowfall, which means more shoveling. It's time to close the window—the room is too cold and getting the flu would be bad. Down the hall the phone is ringing, no answer. The phone rings again, and there are rushed footsteps from the bathroom to the living room to answer. It's not another day in Gitsegukla where nothing happens, not anymore. Throughout the whole village the blare of the fire hall siren can be heard. Not a fire, not some dumb kid trying to burn down an abandoned house or shed. Everyone knows when the siren starts and stops in seven short bursts it means someone died. The door opens and Angie's mother is standing in the frame, eyes filled with tears. That facial expression is familiar. That look had been there when news broke of her grandmother. Angie so worried asking, "Who? Who died mom?"

Angie's mom looks at her daughter, expecting a flood of tears, but she's too stunned. This is an awful dream, or a gag lame screenwriters like to play on the audience. They had spoken on the phone last week; she doesn't believe her mom one bit. Angie picks up the phone to try to call him, no answer. Angie gets dressed and ready to leave. All the while her mom is following her around the house. Angie yells, "Stop!" It's a quick drive up the hill, past the log house, to his driveway. Other cars are parked, and more cars park behind her. Angie slowly opens the door and can hear the sobbing of the women upstairs. She stands at the bottom of the stairway, looking up to where she sees his dad trying to be strong. "Walt's gone," Gilbert's voice breaks, and he walks away beginning to cry. She is confused when these words are spoken. Numb, she walks out the door of Walt's house, looking up and down the street in the tiny village. Something feels so wrong inside her right now, she leans over and starts puking in the snow, except she hadn't eaten so nothing comes out. Eventually, Angie's mom pulls up in the driveway asking if she's okay, but she's not. Angie wants to be left alone and asks her mom to go inside the house. She can hear audible crying when the door opens and closes again. In denial, Angie starts walking out of the driveway, her car blocked in, and slowly makes her way home. The village is buzzing as people are driving around, making their way to his house to try to help in any way they can. Angie thinks she should get back to his house to be with the family, but she wants to go back home. To crawl into bed, to lay on her side, staring at the cordless phone, hoping it would ring. Then when she answered it Walt would be laughing as he did when he pranked her from France. When she sees him again she'll punch him on the arm as hard as she can because this joke is just too cruel.

A plate of wrapped turkey sandwiches and potato chips is sitting on her night stand when she wakes up in the dark, the hallway light is creeping into her room. The living room is quiet except for the beeping of the answering machine. Angie gets up, making her way to it to check the messages, and presses the play button hoping to hear his voice when she presses it. None of the people calling are him. She stares at the answering machine for the longest time. She's not hungry, but forces herself to eat the sandwiches, chips, and a soda from the fridge. Every once in a while, she forces herself to breathe. Sometimes she forgets, and it feels like she's drowning and needs air. She needs some goddamned air.

It's a long walk up the hill. The road is much worse in January when the surface is permanently icy. Now, the November snow is crunchy and soft underneath her boots. She sees two kids racing towards her. Small and innocent, oblivious to the fact that cars often use this road, but here they are happily sliding on their sleds. Angie turns around and sees them crash into a snowbank. They pick themselves up and start running past her, going for another run down the hill trying to get as many rides as they can before they get called home. Walt was so much crazier when he used to go sledding. Angie remembers him veering off the road, hitting a high snowbank, doing a crazy twirl in the air, and landing on his head. Each time someone asked about that scar underneath his eye he'd invent some fantastical lie about its origin. Sometimes it would be an epic knife fight with a squirrel in the forest. Other times it would be a dark wizard who tried to kill him with his wand for not using turn signals. Or worse, the scar manifested when he heard a bad cover on the radio of a folk song he used to love. Each of those stories made Angie laugh, and she smiles remembering that now and feels tears running down her cheek. It hits her, not hard, but still a blow. All she has now are memories. She won't be seeing him this Christmas. They won't go sliding down the icy hill or throwing snowballs on New Year's Eve. She tells herself to just breathe.

The lights outside his house are off, no cars or trucks are parked, and there's no glow of a television on in the living room. Angie knocks gently on the door—no answer. She digs in her pocket for keys, steps inside, and makes it farther than she did earlier in the day. She waits at the bottom of the stairway for anyone to appear, but nobody is coming. After taking off her boots Angie walks slowly up the stairs. She sees his bedroom door is closed, and she peers in the next door through the crack and sees Denise sleeping. The living room is lit by only one lamp, the room painted with a faint orange glow. Stephanie is sitting on the couch and closes a photo album, gets up and hugs Angie without saying anything. They both stifle their crying, trying not to wake Denise. While Stephanie looks through the childhood photo album again, crying as she flips through the pages, Angie goes to the kitchen to make them both a hot cup of tea. They flip through page after page of memories.

Nobody knows what happened to Walt out there in Toronto. An autopsy was being done to determine the cause of death. Unofficially, his roommate tried waking him up, but he wasn't budging. When they checked to see if he was breathing and discovered he wasn't, they called 911. When the doctor pronounced him dead they returned to the dorm searching for a phone number. They broke the news to his dad. Walt's dad asked his brother to ring the seven sirens at the fire hall across the street. Stephanie asks, "Do you think he killed himself?"

Angie doesn't have an answer, she doesn't know what to say, but her gut instinct reply is, "No, he'd never do that. If he couldn't talk with me about stuff, he'd definitely reach out to you if he was in trouble."

Angie asks where everybody is. She learns that everybody went with Walt's parents to the airport, and they are flying out to identify the body and make arrangements to bring him home. Angie's mom drove them using their truck. The two don't talk much that night. Angie tries to comfort Walt's sister as best as she can until she falls asleep crying with her head on Angie's lap. The house is quiet. Angie rests her head back against the cushions of the couch, listening to the grandfather clock ticking away, counting each click with her eyes closed. This bit of calmness will soon pass. Everyone will be busy spending the next week making preparations for the Memorial, Funeral, and Settlement Feast the Gitksan people observe when someone passes away.

Smoke Feast

The wipers on the car let out a rubbery squeaking noise as they brush the snow to the sides of the windshield. Angie has been sitting there in the van for forty-five minutes parked outside the funeral home. Walt's parents spent two days in Toronto making arrangements to bring him back home. They waited for the autopsy, boxed up and shipped home his belongings, and flew the body back. Inside the funeral home the body is dressed in a suit, the casket selected, and a payment plan finalized. Angie, waiting with her mom, adjusts the heat coming out of the vents as she rolls the window down. Though she didn't roll the window down, since cars don't have those anymore, so she pushed the button instead. She puts her hand out and watches snowflakes land and melt in her palm. The three of them sit silently waiting like everyone else. Angie searches the glove box for her mom's hidden stash of leftover Halloween candies, but they're all gone. Michelle, in the backseat, looks around counting all the cars lined up on the street waiting for the procession to start. Angie's mom is eating a fish sandwich. Stephanie asked if they wanted to come inside, but the small funeral parlor was filled with grieving relatives, so they waited outside. Angie sees Stephanie in the truck ahead of her as she entertains little Denise. The weather isn't grim, but it's not perfect, either; it has been trying to snow all morning, but stops after a short spell. Angie's mom knew in advance that they'd be here waiting and offers the two sandwiches she stole from the platter she made that morning. Angie opens the wrapper and is disappointed. The canned salmon sandwich doesn't have any onions in it, just a healthy mix of mayonnaise that makes it sweet when she bites into it. Staring at the entrance to the funeral home Angie sees her former classmates, Walt's best friends, who are the pallbearers. They all look uncomfortable wearing their suits, and occasionally they laugh remembering some odd story or quirk about their friend when he was still alive. Angie looks down at her pants and sees spilled flakes of salmon and quickly eats them before anyone notices. The men go inside, people up and down the street exit their cars, and everyone gathers around the entrance of the funeral home. Angie feels her stomach turn as she stands with the group on the sidewalk, next to Stephanie and Denise, a preview of what will happen in several days. Walt's friends carry him out of the funeral home in the casket. They proceed to his godfather's truck and carefully load the casket in the back, securing it for transport. As that is done everyone files into their respective cars, turn on the engines, and begin the long drive home, all following a pilot car that sets the pace. Angie still trying to be strong blinks away a tear in her eye and swallows a lump in her throat, and she hands Michelle a tissue for her face. Angie presses the hazard button on the dashboard, and the familiar blinking noise it makes fills the cabin of the van. The procession home begins.

It is a quiet trip, a slow trip out of Smithers, as they all make their way onto Highway 16 West. At the front of the line is an uncle in the pilot truck who sets the pace well below the posted speed limit. They're all bringing home precious cargo. Following the pilot car are Walt's godparents with the casket in the back protected by a white fiberglass canopy. In the next car Angie sees Walt's family ahead of them. Both his mother and father are in the front seat, and in the backseat his sister Stephanie, his niece Denise, and his grandmother. Angie sees them visibly distressed, probably crying like Michelle behind her. It takes two hours to make the trip from Smithers to Gitsegukla whenever a body is brought home. Michelle gets uncomfortable when she realizes Angie is looking at her through the vanity mirror and pauses her crying. Except Angie isn't staring at her—instead she's trying to count the cars behind them. When they get to a straight stretch of road she makes it to thirty-three cars with their hazard lights on. Interspersed with those in mourning are regular cars and an odd semi-truck unlucky enough to end up in the convoy. This is how it's always been done when people pass on, this long, slow drive home. Angie looks out at the snowy landscape and presses her finger against the cold foggy passenger side window writing, "33."

Jolted from a daydream memory of Walt, Angie looks up as the van swerves when hitting a patch of grooved wet snow, and her mom apologizes. Michelle laughs nervously, but soon goes quiet thinking she has disrespected the body. "I used to bug him in elementary school," Michelle says, "always asking if he loved me, and if he wanted to get married. I wasn't serious, it was just something that embarrassed him and made his cheeks red. I hope I didn't make him too shy because of that." Angie thinks how introverted her cousin was, keeping to himself, and how he took a long time to warm up to people. She only recently learned Walt hadn't spoken until he was four and had to take extra speech classes on the side. Angie liked to think those extra years Walt was inside his head helped make him become especially creative in the things he did. Some would be quick to diagnose that as a form of Asperger's. Angie tries to hold in a laugh, into her head popped the two words, "ass burgers."

When the line of cars reaches the two-lane passing section of road Angie looks around to see why the cars or semi-truck haven't passed them yet. It's then she sees they have their hazard lights on, too, and the procession has grown even longer. There are no road rage drivers out today, which makes Angie thankful. In the past there had been cases where people impatiently pass all the cars extending their middle fingers, shouting out the window swearing, "Indians," as they sped by. That happened years ago. Angie is grateful there was no repeat of such a shameful display of racism today.

The procession is now passing through "town." Everyone in the surrounding area calls Hazelton "town." Angie sees curious faces looking at them as they pass by the grocery store where Walt used to work. They next pass by the Chinese food place she used to eat fried rice with Walt and Michelle on the weekends. Now in cell tower range texts start coming through on their phones. Michelle and Angie answer them, updating people on how far they are from Gitsegukla so people can make preparations for the arrival in half an hour. People back in the village prepare to get the coffee ready, arrange cookies and snacks, and have the sandwiches ready to serve. Angie's mom turns on the VHF radio to hear random ladies broadcasting their location, reporting that they're now leaving Hazelton, then, after she's heard enough, turns it off.

The procession is now passing the frozen Seeley Lake, with the iconic pointed mountain, Roche De Boule. Angie remembers taking pictures with Walt here during the summer three months ago, both of them hoping one of their shots would be used by the weatherman on the nightly news. Soon after, the procession passes the four crosses, a scene of a bad car accident fifteen years earlier. People lost so much that one night. Three days ago, she lost him.

Butterflies are in her stomach as they climb the hill at Carnaby. Angie knows what will happen next. This happened before when her grandmother died, when they buried the four crosses, and when her basketball coach died on the coast. Now it's Walt's turn. The procession slows down as they descend the hill approaching the bridge, and going under the overpass. The cars tour through the village, passing Angie's house, then turn up the hill toward the white church, crossing on top of the highway overpass, past the log house, past Walt's house, and up the hill towards the community hall. Everyone stops and parks as neatly as they can in the recently plowed parking lot. Walt is now home.

Everyone is silent and they stand in the cold, snow still trying to come down. The men carry the casket into the elementary school gym, which serves as a community hall after hours. Each person makes their way to their respective Clan tables as they wait for the formal announcements. The Smoke Feast is about to begin. When hosting a Feast it is always the mother's Clan that serves. Walt belonged to the Grouse Clan, so all the members of his Clan chip in to hand out the informal snacks and sandwiches after everyone has settled at their tables. The Smoke Feast isn't as elaborate or formal as the funeral Settlement Feasts. Angie notes this as the tables aren't draped in tablecloths—they are bare like they would be if a Bingo was taking place. No one is wearing their regalia at this Feast: no button blankets or vests, no traditional head dresses. Soon Angie is served a soda, a sandwich, and cookies by one of Walt's aunts assigned to serve her Clan's table. Soon after, cartons of cigarettes are opened and packs given to each person attending, which is why the event was called a Smoke Feast. No cigarettes are ever given to minors. It's a small form of payment to everyone attending. The family formally announces the schedule of events relating to the death to take place during the next few days. The head of Walt's house Clan steps up to the microphone with a paper in hand and reads its contents. Several days from now the Memorial will be held in this hall. The next day, the funeral service will happen in this hall because the church is too small. Several hours after the funeral the Settlement Feast will take place. It makes Angie sad thinking there are only a few short days that her cousin has left above ground. Only a few short days making preparations for the Memorial and Feast.

The Smoke Feast is a short affair, and people pack up the assorted snacks and cigarettes that were distributed. The casket is brought out of the community hall and back into the truck, and everyone brings him down the hill to his parent's house. Everyone is in tears when his friends carefully bring him upstairs to the living room—the house is filled with grieving relatives and friends of the family. Angie takes a break from how busy the house is to go down to her house briefly. She sits on her mother's couch and cries a little so nobody can see her. Angie quit smoking last spring, after Walt bugged her about the habit, and she leaves the smokes she was given on the kitchen table for her mom.

First Night

Angie hears the creaking of the floor as another person approaches, stops in their tracks, and turns around, heading back to the living room. Nobody is rude enough to knock—they're just hoping she'll be done soon. The huge reception caught the family off guard. There are many guests in this decent-sized house, and not enough chairs for everyone. Angie looks at the foamy yellow cake, on the paper plate next to the sink. They've run out of cookies and biscuits and resorted to serving store-bought snack cakes. Angie can smell the sweet cake, imagining the sugary center. Locked away from everyone, she knows she will have to exit allowing someone else relief. Angie realizes it's not sanitary to bring food into the bathroom, but it was given to her when she went to wash her face. She's decided to stop wearing makeup for the next couple of days. Angie opts to not eat the cake, a little rule she made up in her head now.

Peering toward the mirror, she doesn't see a reflection. Angie is not a soulless vampire. Like her rule about not eating the cake, his family is observing the rule about not having exposed mirrors in the house when the body is present. For the next week, all the mirrors in the house will be covered with sheets or towels. Angie can say it now. "You're dead, and you died." Angie now grinds her teeth, a reminder that her mouth is closed. His casket is closed. The family hasn't decided if they will allow a viewing of the body before the funeral. Angie is not ready to see him in there. She begins thinking about the mirror again, was this a new custom introduced when mirrors were brought over? If he was here in ghost form visiting and saw his reflection would he get stuck in some hellish purgatory forever? Angie remembers being told to shut up when asking about car mirrors when she was eight years old, *do those not count?* It's just then she decides not to use the car anymore, to not risk Walt's spirit being stuck in the mirror of her old jalopy. "You deserve so much better."

Angie takes a bite of the cake, breaking her made-up rule, and it is too sugary. Opening up the cabinets under the counter she finds standard bathroom cleaning supplies, a few magazines, and spare toilet paper rolls. She once had the crazy idea that if she crawled underneath her bathroom cabinet in Vancouver she could step out and be at her grandmother's house in the village. Angie wonders if Walt had similar ideas too. Closing her eyes, she sees him briefly, laying peaceful, hands crossed, in a nice recently bought suit.

Her ears don't recognize the sound coming out of her mouth. Something inside her is yelling out, "No!" Her hands are clawing at the doorknob struggling to turn it open. Angie falls face first, tripping over herself onto the carpet feeling the sting of rug burn on her right cheek. She's not yelling anymore, it's a mutant wailing sound. The vomit coming up tastes like pancakes to her after eating assorted cookies and sweets, and it starts pooling around her mouth as she lays there numb on the floor.

Stephanie is the first to arrive, muttering, "Oh my god," as she steps into the bathroom to grab a towel.

Angie briefly hopes Stephanie didn't take the towel from the mirror. Angie's mom comes next, trying to keep her hair out of the sick mess. This is the part where the scene ends and everything is neatly resolved so she can shrug off whatever the hell happened to her, she hopes. A part of her wishes she would black out and wake up without this drama. That doesn't happen, that would be too easy.

Angie is helped downstairs by her mom and Stephanie. Stephanie begins cleaning the floor—Angie wants to apologize. Angie and her mom sit on the downstairs couch away from everyone. Her mom asks what happened. Mumbling incoherently, she finally expresses grief, the mental image of her favorite cousin, her almost brother, lying there in the coffin. Stephanie comes down with mouthwash and water. They try as best as they can to clean the puke from Angie's hair, suggesting she should probably take a shower down at her house. Angie then leaves via the front door and walks across the street to pick up a soda and is greeted by Michelle. "What the hell are you doing here?" Michelle hugs Angie to comfort her; she could only take the afternoon off, but still had to work tonight at the gas bar. Michelle asks how the family is doing, then tells Angie that she plans to visit after work. Angie wishes Michelle would start school already and join her in Prince George.

The two step onto the patio, Angie happy to air herself out, but unsure if Michelle can smell the sick on her. It still makes her nervous that Michelle smokes so close to the gas pumps, and Angie says, "One of these days you'll blow us all to hell."

"Would that be such a bad thing?" Michelle asks.

Angie isn't sure if she's serious or joking. Both are hurting too much to delve deeper, so they quietly laugh it off.

Angie notices the brand Michelle is smoking, "You don't smoke that."

Michelle replies, "Smoke Feast—free smokes are free smokes."

Inside, the former TV doctor is playing spin the bottle, but the volume is muted. Angie and Michelle sitting on a used hand me down couch are barely watching the movie. The couch looks like crap, has patches here and there, and a fabric pattern several decades too old, but is so comfortable. Michelle catches Angie off guard asking, "If we were in an indie movie, which one of us would be the one with the mental illness?"

Angie replies, "What?"

Michelle explains most new indie movies have a main character that has a mental illness, conveniently vague, something that allows them to make others uncomfortable, but is also endearing. They ultimately meet a quirky love interest making everything better.

"Life isn't like that, Michelle. People with mental illnesses go see doctors and get medicine."

Michelle coldly replies, "Not around here they don't.

Around here, medicine comes in 24 packs with wild animals for logos."

When the time seemed right, Angie told Michelle that Walt died in his sleep. The coroner's report said as much. Some in the village assumed he was murdered, pushed onto the subway tracks or sacrificed by a cult. It was sleep apnea, and he stopped breathing at some point in the night. Angie thinks about him again, hoping he found his way home, that he's not a lost soul out there in faraway Toronto. She wishes that maybe her deceased grandmother warmly greeted his spirit back to the village, or his grandfather he loved so much.

Michelle starts talking about the creaking noises she sometimes hears at night. She believes her *Ye'eh* (grandfather) visits her *Jüts* (grandmother) from time to time. "When he's ready he will check in on you and make sure things are okay. Our people don't go to hell or get lost in purgatory. This land is our home and we all come back here. I leave a cup of tea on the table sometimes for him, my *Ye'eh*." Angie is comforted by that idea. Better than the extreme white beliefs her dad forced onto her through the church.

Michelle seems ready to ask about the tip of Angie's hair that she noticed has dried chunks of something on it, but a customer comes in the door. Michelle gets up, asking her usual question, "What the hell are you doing here?" She's gotten in the habit of saying that to everyone. People line up for gas, and she puts on her coat to begin fueling up people's cars and taking their money. Angie grabs the earphones Michelle was listening to before. A happy reggae song is playing. Angie tries listening, but the hopeful, upbeat tone rubs her the wrong way. Instead of being comforting, it feels mocking, so she turns it off. She remembers that is another rule for when there's a death in the community. No music—you can't listen to music from a stereo or in your car. Angie doesn't know why that rule exists, but it must be a general show of respect to a grieving family. Left to her imagination she used to believe it would mean bad luck to disrespect the dead with loud music. Angie begins thinking about the Memorial, what people will be saying, what she's going to say. She hasn't found a cool story or anecdote yet, though Michelle already has hers. Angie gets up and looks out the window at Walt's house across the street. More cars are arriving with more guests paying their respects tonight. She should go home and wash the puke out of her hair.

The house was nearly empty when Angie finally returned. Walt's mother and godmother can be heard crying in the bedroom behind the closed door. Angie says hi to Gilbert on the way in—he smokes outside away from the house ever since Denise came into the world. Angie sits on the couch, trying to process the aching, unrelenting pain that leaves her numb. It comes back again hurting as much as it did the first time, unexpected waves of grief. Angie distracts herself by packing Denise around the house, showing her pictures of Walt. She makes a mental note to archive the videos recorded of him during the past few summers and puts Denise to sleep by reading a story. Does little Denise understand why everyone is so sad in the house now, and that they'll be putting her *Bii'* (uncle) into the ground? She kisses the child, vowing to be there for her, the way he would if he was still alive.

Back on the couch, Angie nods to both of them. He won't be alone this week—there will always be a guardian looking over the casket until the funeral happens. Once in a while one of Walt's uncles takes a walk around the house making sure everything is normal. It has been a long time since anyone was caught, and the punishment is severe. In this little community everyone fears witchcraft being practiced when someone dies, *Halwdelgyet*. Angie's mom told her about this when they first moved back to the village from Vancouver. That when someone dies it presents an opportunity to cast evil magic on whoever you want. It involves tampering with the coffin to cast hateful spells, after which the victim will suffer a major health setback or even death. That is the reason most people don't chew gum these days or get haircuts. People are vigilant of their tissues, flushing them or burning them in their stove fires. Angie heard the suggestion a *Halwdelgyet* spell is the reason Walt died. Angie's grandmother told her fantastical stories of witchcraft being rampant in her day. Of people breaking into a grieving family's home, trying to cast their evil spells, but being chased off into the night under gunfire. Angie tried researching the stories on the internet to see if there were police reports corroborating the accounts. That is one thing in the small community that remains hidden and never discussed. The monstrous behavior is hard for Angie to comprehend. Who would hate someone so much to cast a curse on another person by defiling the body of someone as they leave the world? The two uncles aren't armed for war, but it's clear to everyone they are standing watch.

That level of paranoia and suspicion reminds her of several summers ago when a group of vagrants camped by the graveyard. Three folk not from the surrounding communities set up a makeshift camp—at night they'd light a fire, and according to people in the village, singing could be heard. Soon, people gathered their pitchforks and stormed the graveyard, chasing them out of the community, and out of the village. Angie wonders what would have happened if they were caught. She grew up in Vancouver and always had sympathy for the homeless, knowing that their lives are hard and they need help. But she knew they'd have to be stupid to set up camp at a graveyard. Where was the respect? People still talk about that incident, and others claim they practiced dark magic those brief few nights down there. Every family inspected the graves of their deceased and noted nothing seemed disturbed or out of place.

Angie asks herself is she a believer in those superstitious tales of the old days, fearing evil and the intentions of strangers. Village politics is one thing—she's seen the community tear itself apart every two years when a band council election happens. Families vie for power so they have a steady income for two years, but then are replaced by another family the next election cycle. Angie's parents foolishly ran for council and were accused of trying to scoop up wealth for themselves before moving back to the big city. She knows Gitsegukla is struggling with unemployment, poverty, and substance abuse issues. But she can't see how that translates into modern day witchcraft. Is that related to the cases where the community sees several deaths happening in such a small span of time, within days or weeks of each other? Is it much easier to attribute sudden deaths to the healthcare system? To a few dismissive, racist medical practitioners who do not offer the same level of care as they would to a white person? Angie wonders if that kind of thinking and suspicion will still be around when Denise is older.

Walt's mom, Nadine, has stopped crying, and his godmother has gone downstairs to sleep in the guest bedroom. The two watchmen sit on the couches at the ready, sharing a story of how Walt, when he was seven years old, fought valiantly with a salmon at the river. Walt was able to reel it in with his late grandfather's help and providing a week's worth of food for his family. Angie has never gone fishing, and nobody asks her. The two go quiet and finish the coffee that Angie brewed an hour earlier. Stephanie sits at the desk with her dad. The two are writing in a log book keeping track of the tasks everyone has done so far, making sure they miss no one when it is time to acknowledge their contributions. They make a shopping list for the next day when they travel to Terrace. Angie subconsciously avoids looking at the coffin, but from time to time caught herself glaring at it, not mad or hateful, but wishing this all wasn't happening. She goes into the kitchen to see if she needs to make more coffee, but instead washes the dishes even though Stephanie tells her not to. In between plates she looks up, out through the kitchen window at the closed gas station across the street. It takes her a moment to recognize the stance of two people fighting, two shadows swinging their arms at one another. Angie immediately runs down the stairs and out into the cold night.

It's Peter—why is Peter punching that kid's face? Angie has never known him to be a fighter. He is the nicest person she knows and isn't quick to show flashes of anger. She screams at him to stop, to think about what he's doing in front of his house. Peter stops the assault and tells the kid to get the hell out of there. By then, Stephanie has followed Angie. Peter is near to tears, breathing heavily as he calms himself down to explain, "I heard them, the two of them laughing and joking. He's only been back for one day, and those kids were using him as a punch-line to some joke. I'm sorry this happened and you had to see this, but I would not brush it off and walk to my place. I couldn't." Peter stares at his bloody fist. The two try to invite him to the house to at least wash his hands clean, but he wants to go home. Instead, he offers to come at a respectable hour when he isn't working at the community hall. Stephanie asks who the other kid was, but Angie doesn't know anyone in the newer set of teens that have replaced them. Angie looks down seeing the specks of blood on the snow. With her gloves on she rolls up the blood-covered snow into a ball. Stephanie looks at Angie, worried that she's going to cast a hex on that beaten-up kid. Instead Angie throws the snowball to a far-off cluster of trees that breaks it up when it hits the branches. Angie is dubious of this village's superstitious ways, but to be safe, nobody is getting cursed tonight.

Angie is lying in bed, staring at the clock and trying to go to sleep. It was a long day for everyone, but she's still wired from the fight. "Fall asleep already, get some rest, and start tomorrow anew," she tells herself, but then stops to wonder.

"Anew, who uses words like that?"

Angie hears Walt's voice, "You do, because you're a geek."

She recalls a memory of when the two were studying for the grade twelve provincial exams in the high school library. Angie technically wasn't much of a geek like her cousin and never took the time to debate alien politics on that show he liked to watch.

"You goddamned nerd, I miss you," she thinks as she opens the bedroom window just a sliver this time.

Out there somewhere the dogs are howling, as they have been since the seven sirens. Angie wonders what the dogs are saying to each other—how do they know a death happened? Angie starts wondering about what Michelle said about Walt visiting at night. Why can't she feel his presence? She hopes his ghost is with her tonight—she speaks to him inside her head. Angie closes her eyes, and she hopes that if she wishes for it hard enough she'll get to see him in her dreams. Before she falls asleep she simply asks, "Where are you?"

Visitors

The convoy of cars is smaller, and Angie didn't have to strain her neck counting, as there are only two. In the big blue truck behind them she sees Walt's dad, Stephanie, and Denise. Angie and her mom lead the way as they make the hour-and-a-half drive to Terrace for essential gathering of supplies to prepare for the week, making sure they have enough snacks for visiting guests, tissue for the bathrooms, and as much feast supplies they can fit into the truck and van. Walt's mom, Nadine, is staying behind with her mother, hosting visitors as they make their way into the home. Angie noted Nadine seemed better this morning when she served her a giant breakfast of eggs, toast, bacon, and sausages. She likes her mom's cooking, but Walt's mom can't be beat. It's a quiet ride as they listen to the government-subsidized talk radio—they're about to play nondescript generic acoustic music, but Angie turns the radio off. Even an hour away she still observes the no music rule. Breaking the silence Angie's mom mentions her father will be arriving from Vancouver. It's still a sore subject for Angie, and she bites her tongue. She wants to say, "Maybe he'll bring his new family up here and dump them off, then move to Vancouver to start another family again." But Angie's not mean like that and thinks about that other family. Angie has never met her half-brother or his new wife. She's curious about them, but not enough to accept her dad's invitations to visit. Angie's dad, Greg, and Walt's dad, Gilbert, are brothers, so he is coming up to perform the duties that are required of him. She wonders where he will stay for the week, because the guest bedroom at Walt's house is already claimed. The rest of the ride to Terrace is quiet and uneventful.

Terrace always seems so much busier than the quiet pace you see in Smithers. Angie likes Terrace more because the shopping options are more varied, and she doesn't have to deal with the undercurrent of racism she's experienced in Smithers. She's never had a problem with Smithers' business owners, but some of the customers are awful people. There's a nice, healthy mall that rebounded with the economy that competes with two large big box chain stores at the edge of town. Plenty of food options for lunch and dinner. Smithers is the quicker drive, but not having to deal with backhanded comments from local hicks is nice. Terrace has always been slightly more progressive given its proximity to the First Nations' communities of Kitselas and Kitsumkalum. The Nisga'a people up north do their shopping in Terrace too.

Angie wheels around an oversized cart, picking up stuff off the list Stephanie made, buying vegetables for the pots of soup to be cooked the day of the Funeral, and enough ground coffee to serve guests at the house, and later up at the hall for the Memorial and Funeral Feast. Angie can see her mom on the other side of the warehouse being assisted by a nice man with a pallet jack hauling large stacks of bread and crackers. She makes a mental note of returning to pick up bananas, apples, and oranges too. Every once in a while Angie bumps into one of Walt's aunts who are doing shopping to contribute to the House Clan effort. They have no time to chat, instead hurrying along knocking more items off the list.

Technically, Angie and her mom shouldn't be doing any of the shopping or food preparations. Unlike Walt and his family, who belong to the Grouse Clan, *Bisteh*, Angie is a member of the Wolf Clan, *Laxgibuu*. They are not obligated to shop or gather supplies, but Angie was insistent on helping this week. Walt was a brother to her, he did so much when she hit some low points in her life. It feels only right to her to help where she can. Keeping busy allows her to stave off the depression and sadness. All that is normally expected from Angie is to sit at her Clan table at the Funeral Feast and witness everything that unfolds that evening. Walt's parent's pseudo-adopted her when things between her parents were unravelling. They provided her with a safe home to escape to when the drinking got bad and the fighting got worse. Angie catches up with her mom, and they pay several hundred dollars for everything they've purchased. There's a lot of space still left in the van and truck belonging to Walt's father.

Everyone sits in the dark corner of the Chinese food place near the hospital. Walt loved coming here. His dad tells baby stories about him as Denise restlessly fidgets in the toddler chair, banging car keys on the table and laughing. Angie rubs the top of her head, giving a kiss before going outside for air. She is soon joined by Gilbert who sneaks away for a smoke. The two briefly wonder what the score is for the hockey game. The first chance they've had to touch base since the sirens.

Walt's father asks, "Are you alright, Angie? Don't worry

about me or Mom, we're fine, or trying to be."

Something in his voice when saying that causes Angie to hug her uncle. Gilbert has always been a joker, teasing her throughout the years she's really known him, and his current seriousness is alarming. Mostly because it reminds Angie of her actual dad who's probably pulling in to the village at that very moment. Angie wishes her fun uncle would return, to tease her about boys and getting pregnant, or making bad puns with Gitksan words. His favorite expression the past year was, "Everyone likes it up the Nass." The Nass being the river where the Nisga'a people live.

The ride home is long and quiet. While they were enjoying dinner a heavy snowfall started, and the government-contracted plow team hasn't hit the highway yet. Instead, Angie's mom carefully follows the trail a semi-truck is making, getting stuck in the grooves its tires leave. Angie silently thinks about what it would be like living in a big city again. She moved away just as her teen years started, and lived a sheltered life as a child in Vancouver. Prince George is still on her mind. Wanting to get back to school, to see her friends and dorm mates again. School is on hold as the teacher's strike goes on for a third month, but everyone hopes things will resolve by December. She wonders if Walt was happy out there. Did he get to do big city things with his friends and classmates? Did he miss the quiet of the village, playing street hockey with friends, or going to bingo with his sister?

Dogs are often a problem in the village. When the owners don't keep them tied up they are free to reproduce even more dogs, or make a mess of people's garbage bins. Someone is generally hired to round up the strays to take them to shelters in Prince George for adoption or worse. Angie did a research paper on third world countries. It struck her that it's a poor situation when malnourished dogs go wild, form their own packs, and become a menace to society. Thankfully, Gitsegukla dogs are still domesticated and docile. At least the dogs scared off the wild black bear that was encroaching on the village boundaries last summer.

In the winter the village doesn't look so poor, so *Gwe'eh*. The snow takes care of any discarded trash or cigarette butts, and the barren landscaping of people's yards is hidden away. The snow covered soccer field looks inviting in the winter to be torn up by snowmobiles. But that's one thing everyone has decided should be preserved. Soccer is a big deal in the summer months, as the community hosts a grand tournament at the end of May. No one is allowed to ride their snowmobiles on the playing surface of the field. In the village, the Christmas lights make most of the houses cozy and inviting. A few people opted to keep them up year round and not have to deal with the hassle of taking them down and putting them up again. Angie and her mom pull into the village, passing a pair of kids trying to roll a giant snow ball for a snowman. Approaching Walt's house Angie sees the pallbearers have begun helping unload the stuff from the back of the truck into the basement. They'll quickly start on the van when they park. It's that community spirit that she likes about Gitsegukla—its people will always try to lend a hand where they can. Angie makes her way to the basement and sees the massive haul of food and supplies they picked up now stacked in the corner by the pool table. Day one of supply gathering—they'll be making another trip tomorrow for more. Angie sits down with Peter and Doug, and they tell her of who all came by to visit Walt. A few of his old teachers showed up distraught, and they even had a moment of silence and memorial for him at the high school. They all asked where Angie was, wanting to catch up with her and offer their condolences. They knew she was close with her cousin.

Angie stares at Peter's wrapped hands. "It's not broken, just sore and cut," he says as he looks at the stacks of white and whole wheat bread. He tells her the story of how he heard the news that morning. Peter slept through the sirens, and instead his brother casually mentions Walt was thrown onto the subway tracks in Toronto. That was the story being told on the community's VHF radio network before Angie's mom set everyone straight and stopped the stupid rumors. "People have a lot of free time to gossip when there isn't anything to do," he says after he cracks open a soda. Peter declares he should check on his aunt and make sure her stove is full.

Both of Walt's parents come downstairs and join Angie, all commenting on how much more they need to get and dreading the cost of it all. Angie digs her laptop out of the bag to lift their spirits with a video she found and wanted to show. Walt just came back from his summer job and he was sweating in the hot July sun. Angie's off camera voice asks him how his day was and before he could answer, smack, Walt's parents laugh. Stephanie hysterically laughs at having nailed her brother with a water balloon on his forehead and runs down the street before she gets sprayed by Walt holding the lawn hose. The video ends, and it's quiet in the basement. Angie promises to share more as she combs through her computer and phone—maybe she can find material they can use for the Memorial. They go upstairs to sit with the guests who arrived for the evening.

Alone in the kitchen, Angie fishes through the cabinets for a paper plate. She unpacks the brown paper bag she has been carrying with her since they returned from Terrace. She neatly puts the beef fried rice and dry garlic spareribs on the plate. The food is still warm and looks inviting. As other people talk in the living room, Angie starts sneaking downstairs thinking she's alone, but Nadine smiles at her and follows her to the basement. Nadine told Angie how this works, it only makes sense they'd do it together, they will send a plate of food to the other side for Walt to enjoy. Angie stands in front of the wood stove that is emanating heat, the handle warm to the touch. Inside her head, as she closes her eyes, she whispers a quiet prayer, hoping Walt is alright out there. "We brought you your favorite combination dish from Terrace," she says as she opens the stove and gently throws the food into the flames. Both of them hope Walt will enjoy the offering when it reaches him.

Denise smiles as she gets closer to the ceiling, reaching her hands out trying to grab the Christmas decorations her mom hung up last year. It's not long before Denise will try reaching for the dreamcatcher her mom has hanging above the bed. But Angie is careful not to raise Denise so high or that close. Angie puts Denise down on the bed so she can play with her toys she spread out. Angie looks out the window in the backyard of the house. The snow is now a foot deep, except for the brief patch where wood is chopped and a worn trail from the shed leads to the backdoor. The backyard and surrounding house is lit up with the flood lights that were installed earlier in the afternoon, a precaution the watchmen took, protection against supernatural forces. Angie hears voices at the front entrance downstairs. Walt's mom calls her husband downstairs, and there's quiet, concerned talking happening. Angie goes to the door to peek out of Stephanie's bedroom. She sees everyone downstairs putting on their coats and boots. Stephanie sitting at her bedroom desk, asks what's wrong, Angie tells her she will find out.

Outside, the watchman is explaining his routine to them; he goes out every couple of hours and walks around the house making sure no one is sneaking about the property. He shows everyone the trail he has been making in the deepening snow for the past few days. He leads them all to the backyard to the wooded area behind the woodshed. The watchman points east, and they see it. Footprints, fresh, in the snow coming from the wild brush. "Those weren't there before tonight," he says. Everyone is wondering why someone would walk around the house that far off the property. They all head inside, spooked. Not just because the footprints appeared with no one seeing them, but also because they stopped in the clear open field with no sign of backtracking. Walt's dad makes some phone calls, and two more uncles show up in their trucks. One of them has a plow attached to the front of the truck, and he makes a clear road path behind the house. The other uncle parks in the front of the house. Angie's heart beats faster as she realizes they are both armed with shotguns. She's scared at how weird the whole situation is as she explains it to Stephanie. Stephanie watches her uncle plowing a wide patch of driveway that now extends to the back of the house. Angie wonders what kind of person would pull this kind of stunt on the family, and she hopes whoever it is gets theirs in return.

"Give me a shotgun, I'll blow their face off if they try coming back," Michelle says as she takes off her boots at the front door.

Michelle heard the commotion on the VHF radio and came by, concerned. She follows Angie up the stairs as everyone sits around the coffin on guard. Walt's mom jokes with Michelle after she sits down on the couch. "You two were supposed to get married, you know. You kept asking him, and I kept telling him to say yes already." Michelle smiles as his mom continues, "Your granny and his granny approved—it was legal." Not legal in an age sense; they're joking as Michelle & Walt were still little kids. What she meant was that the two belonged to different clans. Michelle's mother and grandmother are Wolves, *Laxgibuu*, and Walt from the Grouse. In the village, elders frown upon people who date others from the same House Clan; it's deemed illegal according to Gitksan law. Coupling with someone from the same house is tantamount to incest. In the olden days it was punishable by death, according to the ancient oral stories they taught Michelle in her youth.

"The problem with living on the rez is that everyone's your cousin," Michelle jokes. Everyone laughs.

The scare has made everyone uneasy—now the family discusses not opening the casket for a viewing and instead, just leaving it closed and locked. Angie listens to the debate with interest, but instead focuses on the large collection of flowers, wreaths, and crosses that have been dropped off as guests pay their respects. She looks at the cards. Angie stops as she reads over the card that Karen sent. "Shouldn't she be here?" Michelle asks after Angie passes it. Karen was Walt's first and only girlfriend—they dated until the end of high school and split up when they went to different Universities. Walt in Toronto and Karen in Alberta. Karen left a teary voicemail for Angie the day she heard the news and expressed how sad she was that she couldn't come home. Like everyone else lucky enough to have student funding from the Education Board, travel money is limited, allowing only enough for travel to school in September, returning home at Christmas, and back home again at the end of the school year. Angie informed Walt's parents of Karen's financial situation and they understand. Michelle begrudgingly accepts that reason, too, and doesn't say anymore after putting the card away.

Now two in the morning, with no other strange occurrences, Angie and Michelle walk home for the night. Michelle stops at the overpass. "My granny cried last night after we got home from the Smoke Feast. She thought maybe when we finished school and came back, my marriage teasing would become real." Angie doesn't know if that's what Michelle wanted. She can't read Michelle's mind. But Michelle and

Walt had great chemistry and had fun teasing each other when they hung out. Michelle continues, "My granny said it's okay to talk to him at night. It will not bring evil to our house if he visits. Have you talked to him?" Angie explains she burned his favorite food earlier in the evening. Michelle excitedly says, "He'll love that. My granny is making *Hashbadinner* and fried bread; we'll put it in the fire for him." Angie wonders how *Hashbadinner* got its name, not sure if it's an actual Gitksan word, but she knows it tastes delicious. The way mashed potatoes and fish, soaked in salt water, gel together perfectly is making Angie hungry thinking about it.

The two arrive at their houses and say goodnight. Angie can hear her mom snoring, but not too loudly. Angie loads up the dishwasher and cleans the kitchen before going to her bedroom. There's still no sign of her father, and she wonders where he is and is hopeful his trip back was safe. She crawls into bed dead tired, the house quiet again except for the hum of the dishwasher. She assumes her mom turned on her side when the snoring stops. "Hello, are you out there?" she asks, but no one answers. Then she sees it, a light on her nightstand illuminates, a message on her phone. She races over to it, hopeful it's from Walt. Michelle is only texting Angie, "Goodnight."

The sun shines directly on the side of her face. She won't get sunburn, but turns to get out of the light. Opening her eyes, she sees Denise standing in her doorway—her hair is especially curly this morning. Little girl will grow up and break a fair share of hearts. Angie waves and smiles at her, pulling back the covers, expecting Denise to join her for an extended nap. They can nap while Stephanie and Angie's mom do whatever they need to do before going to Terrace for more feast supplies. Angie will also make a trip to pick up the wreath and flowers she ordered, to give on behalf of her and her mom. Denise doesn't accept the invite, and she turns around and runs down the hallway with her feet pattering on the linoleum floor. Angie can hear the television on, but can't make out the show, it's just a mumble of voices. She gets up, then stops in the bathroom to wash her face and brush her teeth. It's then she notices she doesn't smell any telltale scents of cooked breakfast, so she decides on a quick bowl of microwave oatmeal as she spits out the mouthwash. In the living room nobody is watching the television, so she turns it off. Now she's worried about Denise, wondering where she went. Angie hears the front door open and close.

Angie runs outside to bring Denise back in the house. Even if it's daylight, it's still too cold for a young infant to be running around out in the frozen November winter. When Angie steps outside she sees the snow has begun melting, and she discovers the trail of tiny footprints leading behind her house, and a larger set of footprints beside it. Angie looks up and down the road on her street of the village—it's quiet with no traffic. On the mirror of her beat-up red car is a little brown bird. One of the birds that like to gather on the highway in the winter attracted to the salt the plow trucks spread to treat the roads. The little bird flies away. Calling out for Denise, she makes her way to the backyard following the footprints. She can hear laughter, and she recognizes her mom's voice, then Stephanie's voice, and Denise giggling.

Angie calms down after finding everyone, they're all sitting at the picnic table. Angie's dad 'claimed' that picnic table nearly seven years ago; it's a permanent fixture in their backyard and the center of many barbeques they host in the summer.

Angie sits down at the picnic table, blocking the girl in so Denise doesn't run away again. Everyone goes quiet staring at Angie. Denise bangs a fork against a glass plate, and Angie notices the food, fried rice and dry garlic spareribs. Angie asks why are they all in the backyard, but before anyone answers the little brown bird lands on the edge of the plate and starts pecking at the rice. A simple creature with a yellow patch on the underbelly that Angie will look up to see the species name later. The bird takes off flying past Angie's head, and everyone watches in silence. Stephanie touches Angie's arm and tells her, "Go." Angie is confused—*go where and why?* Angie carefully walks around to the front of the house, trying not to slip and fall. She turns the corner and sees someone standing beside the car, next to the driver side mirror, he is slightly taller, wearing a black winter jacket and toque.

It's only Doug wanting to talk, but things turned sour after the break up and she's not in the mood to see him this morning. Angie briskly walks to the front steps of the house, intending to not say anything. The man turns around from looking out at the street towards Michelle's house. Angie stares at Doug's face for a moment, it's not Doug. "What is he doing here?" she thinks. Her left foot slips on the ice, and she falls forward into the snow. Angie looks up, thankful, thankful that everything up until this point was just a terrible nightmare. He goes to Angie to help. Angie tries to say his name happily, but it comes out hoarse, she clears her throat, "You're here, Walt, you're here!"

Angie is starting to forget the details of the dream, which are fading as she tries to remember, she can clearly recall only his face. She is laying there on the bed trying to rewind and play it in her head again. Angie wishes she could have talked with Walt just one more time, even if it was a stupid dream.

Both Walt's mom and Michelle claim it was the burning that brought him back—giving him a good meal was enough to call him to her dream. Angie was never a religious person, not church going or a believer in the Creator. She was just too…she doesn't know what the word is to describe herself. To Angie, the cultural identity of who she is has been co-opted and commercialized to the point where it feels hokey and like a parody. She doesn't see the effectiveness of hanging a dreamcatcher above her bed like Stephanie does, going on vision quests in the wild is unheard of, nor talking to animal spirits for guidance. That sort of thing, to Angie, is a lazy white man's interpretation of how they see Indians acting when they characterize them in television shows or movies. It was not the culture she grew up in, not an aspect of the Gitksan culture she's experienced. For Angie, culture is observing the Feast system when someone dies and ensuring the burial is respected. And if a *Simogyet* (Chief) name is passed on is done so correctly, and all obligations are met when someone accepts a Chief or Gitksan name. Angie never heard of anyone who could change into animal form. There is no Gitksan dance that can make it rain, and nobody lives in a tipi or igloo. Angie keeps all the doubt to herself when Walt's mother and

Michelle excitedly talk about Walt coming home. It brings them peace his spirit isn't lost in Toronto, but Angie is uncomfortable at being given credit for such a thing. She wonders if it's just a dream, which are a random jumble of things the brain does while unconscious. Angie flashes back to a vivid dream where she was a vampire who flew around in the sky. She dove into the ocean at super speed, grabbed a shark, flew straight up into the air, and dropped the shark into the wide-open mouth of a killer whale. Angie reasons she could have just willed herself to have the dream after having spent the past few days looking at photos and videos of Walt missing one of her best friends, and trying to process the grief.

Angie, lost in her tangent thoughts, is pulled back to reality by a tug on the arm from Michelle. Not saying anything, Michelle points at the sliding glass door. On the patio rail it's hopping back and forth, a brown little bird with a patch of yellow. Angie shakes her head in disbelief, hoping nobody in Walt's living room noticed. Angie wonders to herself, "Are you a bird? Did you get brought back as a Pine Siskin?" The bird flies away. Now are they supposed to believe he's a bird now?

Michelle tugs Angie's arm and asks, "Why are you glaring?"

Angie goes to the bathroom to wash her face and get away from everyone. As she dries her face she can hear cooing sounds, indicating someone has entered the house to visit. As she opens the door Angie finds herself being hugged and feels the trembling of someone crying by her ears. It's Karen—she made it back for the week. Michelle looks at Angie, shrugging and annoyed. Before Karen lets go, Angie can smell cigarette smoke on her. Angie wonders when she started smoking. Karen goes to Walt's mom and dad giving them a dramatic hug, and then she takes the spot Angie was sitting in as she catches up with the family. In the kitchen, Angie begins stirring sugar into her cup of tea before going to the dining room table. The two parents are caught up with Walt's ex-girlfriend, and Walt's mom comforts her as she breaks down crying. Karen has to leave and unpack at her house, but promises to return in an hour or so.

To Angie's annoyance, his parents used her dream as a sign that tonight would be the night. If Walt's spirit came home they will do a brief showing with the casket open after everyone returns from Terrace. Throughout the private family discussion Angie keeps quiet, and Michelle is the only one who noticed the irritated state of her best friend. Angie wasn't angry or mad, she was scared. The thought of seeing Walt in the box made her puke all over herself after the Smoke Feast, and she dry heaved nothing outside the house after the seven sirens. It takes so much to keep it together and not upset the people around her. Being busy with Feast preparation helps, but she's come to realize something about how the community deals with death. That everyone is on hand when the family is grieving: people guard the body to protect it, and people come with snacks and sandwiches for visiting guests. Everyone is around for the procession, the Smoke Feast, the Memorial, the Funeral, and the Settlement Feast. But what about the family afterwards? People go back to living their lives, back to listening to music loudly, to drinking and having fun on weekends. Angie looks around, seeing the house so full of helpful people, but she knows all too well the emptiness the day after the Settlement Feast. She went through the same thing when her grandmother died, of feeling lost and abandoned. Angie doesn't want to imagine how grim and quiet the house will be after they've buried Walt. It's then she decides she will try to be there for his parents, sister, and niece as much as she can until they don't want her any more. They won't be alone after this week has ended, and she will enlist his friends to not be strangers either.

A long afternoon of cruising the aisles of the mega store nears its end. The van is full of items intended to thank those who helped Walt's family during the hard week. Angie and her mother sit in the van waiting for Stephanie and Walt's parents to exit, then stop for a quick dinner before going back to the village. Angie's mom turns up the heat to defrost the windows, then she starts speaking, "I don't know what to believe, myself. I've seen things that don't have explanations. Pictures falling off shelves. Creaking noises in your grandmother's house coming from the attic. Shadows out of the corner of my eyes. Or seeing a white human-shaped fog drift past the house at night going to the graveyard. I'm a sane, rational person, but there's stuff at odds with this modern time." Angie reflects on the dream about the bird. Angie's mom continues, "When you were born, people looked at your then curly red hair and marveled at how you reminded them of my grandmother. When they saw the way your middle toe sticks to your fourth toe they said you were her and came back to our family." Angie's mom never told this story. "Our people return, they don't go away forever. Right now, they need to hold on to hope. It's not so silly to try to make sense of this loss." Angie feels like a fraud, though, ever since making the mistake of sharing the dream. She's not a hero who brought Walt home. Angie shared all of this during the ride to Terrace. Angie's mom recounts her grandmother winning beauty contests way back in the day, "You try to pass yourself off as this normal, intellectual girl but you are absolutely stunning the way she was. You have her big heart, so loving and caring, but also a fire and hunger for life." Angie is embarrassed and tries to change the subject. Her mom goes back on topic, "Your dad and his dad went out there this afternoon, to the back of the house where they found the footprints. They followed them from the woodshed to the woods. The footprints came out of nowhere." Angie sits there stunned, thinking her mom is lying. She wonders did his spirit come home because she burned the plate of food? Did he visit in her dream?

Everyone sits around the table eating dinner at the restaurant. Angie is still thinking about the footprints, distracted. Karen plays with Denise feeding her food and making airplane noises. Stephanie and her dad are making the list of speakers for the Memorial. Under the table, Angie wiggles her toes inside the boots. Is Angie her great grandmother re-incarnated? It reminds her of the book she read about the African spirit child, such a beautifully written book. To her, this life isn't so flowery or well crafted. She pokes her chicken salad with a fork not hungry. Angie is saving herself for a hot plate of mashed potatoes and salt fish Michelle promised to save for when she gets home. Out of nowhere Denise breaks into a hysterical laugh, but Karen hasn't done anything different. Everyone at the table looks at her, then she stops laughing. Angie remembers an eleven-year-old Walt smearing blueberries all over his face and a white pillowcase on his head as a hat, a goofy imitation of the kids cartoon he watched after school with Stephanie so long ago. Angie takes a quick look around the table, and sees that everyone else is remembering a happy memory of him privately too.

The Viewing

She steps out into the cold backyard where she used to make snowballs and throw them up at his window. Angie's way of signaling Walt to let her in so she wouldn't have to listen to her parents drunkenly yell all night. It hurts her when she takes in a large breath of the cold air. Gazing up at the stars she squints, trying to find any passing satellites overhead. Angie needed to take a breath, to take a break from labeling the gift baskets. It hits her that his time is running out. Two more nights under this roof before he is buried with his grandparents. Angie sees the lights up and down the street of the neighbors, and she wonders what they are doing right now. People who aren't praying upstairs or singing Christian songs on guitar, what are they doing out there in the village right now? Are they watching hockey, playing video games, surfing the internet? Angie looks at the woods where the footprints appeared. She thinks as a joke he'd probably show up as a faint blue ghost right now and tell her she needs to start her training. Angie still needs fresh air, so she apologizes to Stephanie and says that she needs to go for a walk. Stephanie understands and doesn't want her cousin puking over everything, but reminds her they'll be opening the casket soon.

For six minutes of cold silence she stands in her spot with no cars driving on the highway to count. It's just her alone in the dark, standing on the overpass. She keeps herself from crying, but once in a while has to wipe away a tear before it freezes on her cheek. "Hi, Angie," says a quiet voice behind her. She turns and sees a little boy, maybe nine or ten years old. She recognizes him from the birthday parties she'd attended with Walt in the spring. It's one of Walt's little cousins, from his mom's side of the family, Eric. Angie asks him what he's doing out so late, and he takes off his toque showing her, he got his hair cut. He tells her he threw the hair in the fire so no one could curse him. Angie comforts him, telling Eric that they're watching the house and have guns, and that he need not worry about such things. "Are you sad?" he asks.

Angie keeps it together, she answers, "Yes."

Eric asks if she's cold, and she repeats her answer.

"Come with me to my Geech's," he offers.

Angie follows Eric to visit Walt's grandmother—he always called her *Geech*. The dogs bark as the two approach the house, and the motion sensor porch light turns on. The two walk in the backdoor into the kitchen; Eric's mom asks to see his haircut and is happy with the result. Eric assures his mom he burned the hair in the fire before coming home. She tells him to go take a shower. Angie unties her boots and sits down at the kitchen table, wiping her fogged-up glasses. Walt's grandmother, *Geech*, looks much better compared to the last time Angie saw her, no longer in pain or discomfort from hip surgery. Angie remembers feeling like an invader in the house, that first time Walt brought her here to visit. But now she's welcome and comfortable sipping a hot cup of tea. It took Angie a long time to warm up to the mother's side of

Walt's family, since they were all strangers to her.

Geech asks how she is doing, if she's okay, saying she knows Angie lost a brother this week. Walt's grandmother says it's always hard losing someone so suddenly, so unexpectedly. Geech starts crying, and Angie gets up and sits next to her, hugging her. It's not long before Angie lets it all out. When they've stopped, Angie sees the coffee table with photo albums on top. Walt's grandmother has been choosing pictures for the slideshow presentation that will happen at the Memorial: pictures of birthday parties they had, Walt sitting happy in between his Geech and Ye'eh, his grandparents, holding a large wad of money up to the camera. Angie looks through the book and finds a picture of Walt and Stephanie riding bikes. The more she flips through the photo album the younger he gets.

The earliest picture of Walt is when he was at Bear Glacier near Stewart, up by the Alaska border, a family trip they had taken every summer. Walt's parents look so young—in their early twenties. Stephanie is a smiling two year old girl in her dad's arms. Walt's grandfather holding the little baby Walt in his hands. Every year the family would go up that way to pick berries, then stop at Hyder Alaska. They even took Angie last summer—her first bar experience after being at the legal drinking age. She sat there eating nachos, drinking beer, and playing pool with Walt and Stephanie. Each year they took the trip up there, stopped at the rest area in front of the glacier, and each year Angie notices that the glacier gets smaller. Geech teases Angie about passing out in the truck as they left Alaska. Angie embarrassed at the memory smiles, and starts laughing when Geech pulls out the photo where Walt and Stephanie had to hold up Angie, standing in front of the icy blue glacier the previous summer. Nobody lets her forget about needing to pee in the bushes near Meziadin Junction where they fill up the gas tanks before coming home. Eric's mom has finished baking the cupcakes for Walt's visitors. It's now time to see him. Geech promises she'll be there for Angie.

The clicking sounds of the casket being unlocked makes Angie wince, even as she intentionally hides away in the kitchen, wrapping plates with foil, saving snacks and sandwiches for when they're needed. It sounds like everyone is crying in the living room. All that pain is unbearable for her to be in, and she considers running downstairs. Walt's mom is surrounded by her sisters and mother as they walk up to the open casket. Nadine looks at her son resting peaceful with a calm expression on his face, eyes closed and hands on top of each other. The suit is black, and he's wearing a white shirt and a striped tie. Angie thought she was done crying, but her mom takes her by the hand and leads her into the living room. Angie stands there beside her mom, looking down and getting lost in grief and tears, uncontrollable tears she can't hide from anyone anymore. In that moment, she feels someone next to her holding her up, stopping her from buckling down onto the floor. She turns and cries into his chest, leaving a mess of tears and a runny nose on his shirt. Angie didn't know she would be so thankful her dad was there. Angie's parents lead her to Denise's room to calm her down and console her. She didn't recognize Walt at first—not without the trademark glasses he had to wear sometimes. But she saw the faint scar underneath his eye and knew it was him in there. After everyone views the body the casket is closed. Angie continues to hide out in Stephanie's room where Denise plays with Angie's hair, wrapping it around her fingers. They kept Denise from seeing her uncle like that. Angie goes to the bathroom to grab a tissue and blow her nose, and on her way there she notices the padlock installed on Walt's bedroom door. That room will never be opened again. She will never hang out there like she used to. And Angie shakes her head to wipe away the frown as she looks at the lock and grabs the tissue before returning to Stephanie's room.

Angie's dad, Greg, knocks on the door to visit his daughter. Stephanie picks up Denise to give the two time alone to talk or catch up. Angie thanks her dad for holding her up as she was breaking down. They sit on the bed, not sure where to start, instead talking of the drive from Vancouver to Gitsegukla. Greg invites Angie to come visit for Christmas. But as always, Angie gives a non-committal answer. She clarifies she wants to be there for Walt's family. Angie wishes things hadn't gone to hell with her dad—she doesn't hate him or his new family. Greg tries to be there for his daughter when he can. He pulls out a photo from his inside coat pocket, an old photo snapped so many years ago, and hands it to Angie. She looks at it, curious; Angie doesn't have a memory of the photo being taken, and she has a knack for remembering everything and recalling memories chronologically. In the photo, they sit in the backseat buckled in. A three-year-old Angie, hair in pig tails, holding hands with Walt, him looking out at the alien

Vancouver skyline. Angie smiles, showing off the gap in her front teeth for the camera. Walt is sucking on a straw from the soda in his hand. Angie's dad says, "Two cousins met for the first time." He hugs her before announcing that he has to leave. Stephanie comes back in with Denise and sits down next to Angie. She glances at the picture, wondering where she was when it was taken, as Stephanie was always inseparable from her younger brother.

The gas station has closed, but Michelle is working, restocking shelves and the fridge with soda. Angie joins her, leaving for the night to get away from the rawness inside Walt's house after the viewing. The two make their way to the back room with the couch and sit down. Angie is surprised that Peter is already there watching hockey highlights on the television. Karen and Doug enter, and everyone sits down after hugging. Angie is still trying to shake the image of her cousin in the coffin out of her head. Seeing Walt in there made it absolutely real. She held on to a hope that he was still in Toronto, working on making computer programs with his friends or watching movies, those childish hopes dashed. Angie sees his house out the window and the lights are off. Everyone is getting an early night to rest and prepare for tomorrow. And only the flood lights and running trucks of the watchmen outside are on. Angie takes a sip from her can of iced tea, and Michelle opens up the mini-fridge and offers everyone a can of beer. This isn't a party—nobody is going to get drunk as it's just a gathering of the graduating class from Gitsegukla two years prior. Everyone but Angie has a beer, but they all barely sip on it, letting it get warm in their hands.

A hockey highlight reminds Peter of the time he was playing goalie in Doug's homemade hockey rink and Walt scored, whipping the puck into the top left corner. Michelle fondly recalls her dragging Walt out to ride on her snowmobile, hitting a jump, and him flying off and landing in the snow face first. Everyone wants to tell a nice story about him, but instead they silently listen to the hum of the freezer that holds the ice cream and frozen microwave pizza.

Peter talks about the old elementary school, asking if they all remember it, which was demolished before Angie moved back home. The elementary school was two joined buildings across from the old fire hall, replaced by the modern health station. It's why there's a big dirt field in front of the band office. It used to be a school field before a newer replacement was built up the hill. "He was always quiet. He'd sit with us in class, but he'd watch rather than talk with us or the teacher, that god-awful teacher," Peter finishes. Karen reminds everyone that Walt didn't speak until he was four. Doug and Michelle remember how they would cry and fight with their parents to try to get out of going to school, pretending to be sick, but they were forced to go. Peter continues, "She was a mean old bitch who shouldn't have been in the classroom. I don't know if she was pure evil or just hated Indians. When we would do kid things like talking with each other or bugging other kids having fun, she'd come up behind whoever she thought was misbehaving and give them a slight pinch on the shoulder, but not enough to leave a mark. I don't remember what I was doing, but I made Michelle mad and she threw blocks at me."

Michelle teases Peter, "You're such a big meanie face."

Peter goes on, "Just as Michelle started to throw something else the teacher grabbed her wrist hard. I remember the squeal Michelle made, part surprise, but mostly pain. Every kid in the class went quiet, staring at the three of us at our table. Then for good measure she slapped Michelle on the back of the head, scolding her and pinched her shoulder, causing her to cry." Angie is taken aback at the story of child abuse. That would not happen these days. Peter finishes, "And we heard him roar, almost literally. Walt got up on his wooden chair and yelled out NO! He kept saying it over and over, getting louder, alternating between yelling NO and BAD until the other kids followed his lead. The teacher stormed up to Walt ready to slap him on the face when the first grade teacher opened the door, seeing the whole scene and stopping the assault. The two teachers left the class, and an assistant sat with us kids reading a book."

Michelle adds, "He was a hero, my hero. The grade one teacher brought us to the office to tell the story to the Principal and administrators. Walt's dad was there, too, back when he served on the school board." The teacher was quickly fired and a kinder, gentler replacement found. Everyone still wonders what happened to that witch, but that's in the past.

Karen asks out loud, "I kind of wonder where that fire came from. What compelled him to do the right thing?" She explains how Walt went out of his way to help others or stand up to injustice, that he often stood up to white bullies in high school who were harassing freshmen natives. He'd never get violent, but confronted them in a way which caused them to stop.

Doug mentions, "Those searing eyes would give you pause if you ever got on his bad side. That alone was enough to make people stop their crap." Karen declares she has to get home and get some sleep, which signals the end of the little gathering. Everyone files out of the gas station and goes their separate ways.

That is the last time they ever saw each other, all together. Michelle got drafted in the war. Peter started a cult and went up the mountain before being arrested by the police. Karen joined the first manned mission to Mars. Angie and Doug fought valiantly against a mutated hoard of zombies. Angie snickers to herself thinking that ending up in her head as she sits on the church steps with Michelle. *You never have friends later on like you do on the rez.*

Angie enters the dark house after hanging out with Michelle, taking off her boots quietly and walking up the stairs. She sees her dad sleeping on the couch, kisses him on the forehead goodnight, then goes to her bedroom. Laying down looking up at the bumps on the ceiling, she waits patiently. The stars start glowing one at a time—little stickers she put up during the summer. She looks for it; she gave him one sheet. Right there, near her closet, is a cat with a big smiley face staring back at her. "Bad cat, making me smile tonight."

Memorial

The echo of chairs being unstacked reverberates throughout the large gymnasium. Angie looks at the fold-away bleachers, wondering how long it was since the hall had hosted a real sporting event? Local artists spruced up the interior walls with traditional paintings of assorted house crests, animals that represent each clan in the community. The black-and-red-painted designs are striking and unique, just like the two-story entrance featuring carved designs in the front of the community hall. From behind her, she hears rusty wheels being rolled her way, and watches the crew set up the speaker's podium on the stage. The speaker system that is normally used to call out bingo numbers will now be used for the multitude of speeches that will be made later on tonight. Angie walks out of the gym, looking out at the plowed parking lot. Up the hill she can see little kids trying to run in waist-high snow across the field, chasing each other. Angie realizes they don't need her in the way. She thought she could be helpful, but instead she walks down the hill to Walt's house, stopping in front of the house and staring at all the parked cars, taking a moment before entering. Peter joins her, holding a large briefcase. He explains it's the projector for the slideshow presentation that is planned. He doesn't have much time to talk and apologizes as he walks up the hill to the school. While looking up at the elementary school, Angie realizes how lucky Walt and Stephanie were to just be a quick run or walk from school and not having to ride a long, annoying bus like she did when she attended school in Vancouver. Not having to worry about being abducted by strangers. Angie realizes she's freezing, presses her soft wooly gloves to her cheeks, and makes her way inside the house.

Instead of going upstairs, where crying can be heard, she walks straight forward to the pool table room. Stephanie is looking over each of the prepared gift baskets, doing an inventory, matching everything up to her list, and eventually sits down with Angie on the couch. Both realize it is Walt's last day in the house. Angie updates Stephanie on how ready the gym is looking and mentions that she met Peter, who is setting up the equipment. Instead of running away from the truth Stephanie begins speaking, "One more day. I can't believe it. I've been so busy with feast preparations and looking after Denise, it's been ages since I've sat down and thought about him." Stephanie takes a break to sip her coffee. "I feel sick, tense, and sometimes I wish I could just walk away from all of this. Denise will never know her uncle as she grows up. I will never meet his future wife, or any of the kids he would have had." Stephanie goes upstairs to check on Denise, leaving Angie. Angie goes across the street, hoping to catch up with Michelle at the gas station. But Michelle got a substitute worker to cover her shift and is nowhere to be seen. Just a young teenage girl reading a book behind the counter. Angie picks up a soda and a bag of chips, and a chocolate bar for Denise.

When Angie returns to Walt's house she goes upstairs. The crammed living room is full of visitors. Family who've traveled from across the region to be there for the Memorial service, many people she doesn't recognize. A line has formed as the guests approach the coffin to see him lying in there. At the front of the line, Michelle is holding her grandmother's arm and clutching a tissue she holds to her face, wiping away tears. Barely audible, Michelle says goodbye to Angie as she leads her grandmother down the stairs and back to their house. Not long after, Karen arrives wearing black pants and a black blouse. She comes alone. Angie offers to stand with her as they view the body. This time, Angie vows to be stronger, and she feels herself holding Karen up at times. After their turn is over she leads Karen to Stephanie's room. Karen upset leans in an upright fetal position crying. Angie can only put her arm around her shoulder. After Karen finishes, she thanks Angie for being there for her. She offers to get Karen coffee and cookies from the kitchen. Angie was never as friendly with Karen as she is with Michelle or Peter; there was a coolness between the two when Karen dated Walt through high school. They sit on the bed thinking what if. What if Walt and Karen both went to school in Vancouver and didn't split up? They were a great couple, without the drama, and were happy together. Karen gets up and tells Angie she'll see her at the Memorial.

Uncles and aunts pop their heads in saying hi to Angie, who hasn't yet left Stephanie's room. She tries to smile and tell them she's fine and asks how they are doing in return. Then she notices the clock, two hours to go before show time. Stephanie brings in Denise to change the diaper. Angie takes this as a cue to go mingle with the guests. She goes to the living room and sits next to her mom, watching people approach the coffin, staring at Walt, saying bye, and leaving solemnly. Angie looks at the large, framed graduation picture standing up next to the coffin. She smiles to herself, remembering the yearbook quote he submitted to be under his photo, "Ishxw Mismoodix Mismuus." People still ask Angie what that means, but she can only smile at Walt's weird sense of humor. A nod to a phrase the Gitksan language teacher taught them way back in elementary school.

Angie tries clinging on to time as much as she can, keeping tabs on the watch near the dining room and making sure not to lose anymore. She stares at his face from where she is sitting, trying to ingrain his image into memory. She never wants to forget his quirky, tiny chuckle, or his boisterous fake laugh as he impersonated a spy movie villain. She wants to hold onto the quiet way he'd assert himself when talking, starting off slightly mousey in what he would say. But the vocal training kicked in and he would enunciate his message with clarity and authority. She'll miss the times he would drop an obscure movie reference or quote, get disappointed nobody got it, and laugh for being clever. Angie still looks at the hallway, waiting for him to come into the room asking, 'Who eats monkeys?' That baffled everyone and he never explained why he'd say that. After Denise was born, he'd ask that question, and use her like a puppet answering the question, 'We eat monkeys!' Angie remembers his quiet sigh. He would raise his eyebrows, look at her, exhale, and the two of them knew what he was thinking and would laugh or smile quietly. Angie closes her eyes, imagines he does that, and she makes a smile and has a tiny laugh. When her eyes open she sees everyone staring at her like she's some kind of weirdo, and she smiles more, knowing Walt would get a kick out of that. And all over again the grief consumes her whole as she cries into her mother's shoulder.

The dress feels wrong. It fits, but it makes her uncomfortable wearing it. Angie has never worn dresses, and she's embraced the jeans-orientated style of the north. Wearing a dress in the winter is foolish, and in the summer an invitation for mosquitos. She puts on the necklace her late grandmother gave—a simple gold chain with a pendant of the Wolf Clan. Looking in the mirror she is technically ready, but wants to go change into something like the clothes Karen wore earlier. She imagines Walt telling her that an alternate universe version of Angie is resisting the clothing, that their entangled selves are in the same space, but would rather be wearing lazy sweatpants and a university sweatshirt. Angie thinks about wanting to open a portal to an alternate universe where Walt is still alive. Instead of going to the Memorial she can take Walt and Michelle to a movie in Terrace. But Angie doesn't know what she's talking about. She's not a physics nerd and is only regurgitating nerd speak picked up watching science fiction shows and movies with Walt on the weekends. Angie goes to the living room, and her parents say she looks so pretty.

Everyone Walt has ever known is now standing in the driveway. The weather changed and it is now snowing, light flakes floating down. The pallbearers carry the coffin outside, being extra careful not to slip or make a mistake. Step by step, they walk down to the truck to load Walt in the back. Pallbearers sit in the truck, holding on for the short drive up to the gym. Angie wonders who will speak tonight. What will be said in his name, in his memory, and in his honor? The slow procession arrives at the front entrance of the gym, and there are people waiting inside sitting down. Everyone follows the coffin into the hall, Angie notes that half the seats are occupied by community members, friends, and teachers from the elementary and high school. A Christian band on the stage plays a song about heaven as the family walks with the coffin to the front of the building. The coffin rests at the base of the stage, with family sitting in the front few rows of the hall. As the band finishes the song, Angie realizes it is the same song played at her grandmother's Memorial ten years earlier.

This Memorial is an extension of tomorrow's funeral. A funeral that will also be held in the community hall everyone now sits in. The church where Walt was baptized, a glorious white church in the middle of the community built by Angie and Walt's grandparents, is too small for everyone who will be in attendance. The service starts with a prayer by the community's preacher. He prays for Walt's family, for strength so they can get through this hard time, for others to be there for the family when they most need it. He prays for Walt, for his spirit to find its way to the next life. Angie looks down at the photocopied program and schedule. She is saddened his graduation picture doesn't have *Ishxw Mismoodix Mismuus* on the front, just the two dates of when he entered and left their lives. Walt's oldest aunt has been chosen to be the MC for the night and invites the band to play another song after the preacher finishes his opening. Angie asks her parents if they want a drink from the concession stand in the corner of the hall, and she goes there still holding onto the program. Michelle follows her as the band plays hopeful music for those that need to hear it. The two girls look out at the full hall, watching people who will sit in hard, stiff chairs for the next few hours. Doug joins the two as he picks up a diet soda. Angie hugs him, thanking him and the other pallbearers for being so careful when transporting Walt. Michelle looks at the program and smiles without laughing, thinking of the absurd graduation quote too.

Seated, everyone listens to stories about Walt from his life as he grew up from a quiet little boy to a scholarship-winning young man who traveled to far away Toronto. There are tales of him playing games with his late great grandmother, of stealing her cane and being chased around the house lovingly. Stories of uncles who took him hunting with his grandfather up the mountain—up the mountain where he no doubt imagined he was going on an epic quest to destroy an unholy object in some volcano. Angie imagines how happy that made Walt, to be living like the stories he would read in his books. Walt's uncle, one of the night watchmen, tells the story of how a man named Albert took Walt on his shoulders and waded waist-deep into a creek. And all the time Walt would make vroom vroom noises. Everyone in the hall falls silent. No murmur of people talking in hushed tones, no kids or babies crying, no weeping. Everyone is in thought remembering Albert briefly and the huge loss the community experienced when he passed. He was a father, an uncle, and a coach to the youth basketball team. Angie thinks, *rest in peace Albert, you are not forgotten.* Other people bring up stories of friends and family they've lost over the years and promise to be there for Walt's family if they need someone to talk or cry to. Teachers speak of how bright and creative he was, a good student, with so much life ahead of him.

Angie's friends take the stage in turn. They bring up stories of growing up with Walt, of how great a friend he was to them throughout his life. They're stories she has been hearing this week, and she realizes some of her friends were practicing for tonight. Everyone who has told a story walk off when they finish and look at him in the open casket and whisper their goodbyes. Karen speaks of their love, of what a good man his parents raised. Doug brings up hilarious pranks they used to play on their parents, telling the story when they were in France and pretended to be arrested by the police. Everyone in the hall laughs or chuckles at the made-up charge of peeing off the Eiffel Tower. Michelle talks about the flirting, the teasing, the planned marriage, and then mentions the pinching teacher story that makes some people in the crowd uncomfortable. Before she finishes she holds up the Memorial program, explaining to those who don't understand the Gitksan language yearbook inscription he chose, *"Ishxw Mismoodix Mismuus."* The crowd laughs when they hear it. "For the *Amshwa,* or those that don't speak Gitksan, The Cows Tits Stink." She laughs and then finishes, "He was a great guy, a protector, he was funny, and always a friend. I'm going to miss you so much, Walt."

Angie isn't watching the clock anymore, but she soon finds that nearly four hours have passed. The night quickly passed by as people tell their stories, sing their songs, and offer condolences to the family sitting at the front of the hall. After every person speaks they shake the hands of the family out of respect before returning to their seats. A slide show presentation featuring childhood photos of Walt plays next on the screen. A visual document of his life from when he was just a baby boy being held by his parents and grandparents—all the way to the last time they hugged him at Vancouver airport two and a half months prior. Angie has not spoken yet. She was supposed to lead the graduating class before all his friends spoke. She's nervous before the large crowd, not knowing what to say. Peter offers to take her place, and she is immensely grateful. The intermission is about to start, and people will go fill up their coffee, get new sodas, or take a quick smoke break outside. Walt's aunt approaches Angie, asking if she's ready to talk yet—she looks at him in the casket and answers, "Yes. I will."

Angie brings a paper cup of water to the podium. She's nervous and can almost swear she feels sweat forming on her forehead. Inside, she has a jumbled mess of good memories that she wishes she could say out loud all at once, coherently. Angie looks around the full hall. She clears her throat, conscious of her dress, which feels airy because the vent behind the stage is pumping warm air that faintly brushes against her ankles. She wonders why she didn't just wear winter boots like everyone else. Looking down at the coffin she begins, but is surprised by her voice—it sounds too loud so she eases off from the microphone:

Walt, I don't remember us meeting for the first time back in

Vancouver. I don't remember riding a train, or staring at a killer whale, or walking along the sea wall in Stanley Park. Those are stories people have told me of when we were just little kids. This is us. I apologize, I should have had this picture scanned into the computer for the projector. It's a photo of the two of us meeting for the first time in Vancouver when we were three or four years old. There are so many stories of us that make me laugh, bring me joy. But these days the memories make me cry so much that I can't stand on my own feet, because I know they're all I'll have left after tonight and tomorrow. I honestly can't bring myself to say goodbye—I thought we'd have more time. Time for memories, of things shared, of life lived. Everyone here carries with them a piece of you that brings them happiness, but also, for now, sadness. This—what's happening now isn't fair. It isn't fair to your mother, your father, your sister, and your little niece. To all of us that loved you so much. Tonight, we are trying our hardest to celebrate your life as best as we can. To remember you and keep you in our hearts. It hurts so much standing here seeing you down there. I don't remember us meeting for the first time, as that is one of those blurry memories from when I was this snot-nosed kid. Instead, this is what I remember.

There I was, in the dead of winter, standing on the overpass, freezing cold, counting trucks. Because that's what us cool kids do here on the reserve on a Friday or Saturday night. It wasn't a Friday or Saturday night; it was last night. Out of nowhere I hear his little voice. He asks me how I'm doing. If I want to come visit your Geech, your grandmother, and warm up. I should know better than to just stand in the freezing winter, but it's been a hard week, and I was taking time to myself. I don't remember what I was thinking about. Last night feels so long ago. Then your awesome little cousin Eric comes along and invites me home to warm up and prevent a cold. I had a good night last night with your grandmother. It's weird that it happened again, almost exactly to the letter, like the first time I met you, cousin, my friend, my brother.

I don't want to put anybody on the spot. What happened in the past is done and over. Things weren't as good as they could be when I was fifteen. And it's like that for most of us in this village, but we make it through as best as we can. It was a cold night, and I went for a walk. I walked around this whole village. Up to this school, down to the band office, by the Church, past my house, and back up to the overpass. I stood there for half an hour, counting cars and trucks. Thirty-three was how far I got. In that time, people would walk by. Some people I sort of recognized, but didn't know too well. And they would say hi as they went to wherever they were going. Alone with my thoughts, counting traffic like some weirdo nerd with too much time on her hands. And it's true I am sort of a weirdo nerd, but that's okay. You got me, and I got you. Your odd jokes or pop culture references. All of that would not have come to be if you weren't the good person you are—were.

Maybe your spirit nudged your cousin to say hi last night. I rarely think of ghosts or spirits, or of coincidences and fate. They say you've come back and you're not lost out in Toronto anymore. I hope it's true. That for the past week you've been hearing what I've been trying to say to you in my head. And you're here right now. You've heard all the loving recollections everyone has of you—that you are sorely missed. Sometimes I try to listen for you at night to see if you're with us, or if I can feel your presence. I don't. I had a dream about you, and it was so bittersweet after I woke up. Like that, again, I lost you.

There you were, nearly six years ago, walking home on a cold night, and you see this strange girl counting cars on the overpass. You stopped, you asked her if she wanted to play pool or darts. Just that quickly you changed a life. A life where that weird, awkward girl wasn't so alone anymore. She had a safe place to be when things were rough. A life where she made it through the darkness, a life where I found good friends to grow up with, and even a life where I knew love. You stopped that night, and we met for the first time. To my parents, I apologize for bringing up old wounds; I know both of you weren't happy, but I'm happy that you are now. I wasn't out there counting cars or hiding away from things. I was making my mind up about jumping off the bridge. I was hoping the impact would be quick and painless. That I wouldn't drown in the cold Skeena River. And the hurt that dumb, weird fifteen-year-old girl had back then would end. For whatever reason, that didn't happen. He stopped, he said hello, and he saved my life. I am here now because of you, Walt. I wish that I could have been there for you that night in Toronto, that I could have saved your life in return. Mom, Dad, Walt's family, I'm sorry for bringing such a thing up, here of all places. I see the worry in your eyes. That was a different person back then standing on that overpass, a person who hadn't met him just yet. This life, my life, was saved from a pointless, tragic end. Walt, I will live for you. I will go to school and find a career. I will hopefully find happiness, maybe love, and way down the road from now I'll have little kids that will be best friends with your niece Denise. Who knows? Walt is the reason I am here right now, standing on this stage and telling this uncomfortable story. That is how he changed my life. If you are out there, if you can hear me, I just want to say thank you.

Angie walks off the stage, and it is silent in the whole hall. Everyone looks at her with concern and worry. She stops and turns and looks down at him once more, then whispers a quiet thank you. Angie closes her teary eyes and pictures hugging Walt one last time. Just as she did when they dropped him off at the airport. Angie sits down between her parents and Walt's parents. She'll be okay. Wherever this life takes her, it is because of him.

The procession of cars return the body to the house, and it is Walt's last night under his own roof. Only family are allowed to enter as people sit in the living room guarding Walt. It was a long Memorial service; it finished at 12:45 in the morning. Everyone has to wake up early for the funeral and to start cooking soup for the feast. Angie sits in Stephanie's room alone, looking at his picture she keeps on the desk. A knock on the door sounds. It's Michelle, and she joins Angie sitting on the bed. Angie explains to Michelle, "What's said is said, and I meant it. I am no danger to myself, not anymore. I was a dumb, stupid teenager back then." Michelle believes her. Angie needs to go home, change, and get out of the alien clothes. Angie's parents come in the room to pick her up, to take her home. Before they all leave they take one long look at the coffin. Michelle grabs Angie's hand and leads her down the stairs and into her mom's van.

Changed and now in pajamas Angie sits on the couch for half an hour, explaining to her parents that what she said is in the past. She's annoyed, but understands their concern. Michelle joins Angie in the bedroom. Michelle grills Angie more bluntly, "I just need to know tomorrow afternoon will be the last time, for a long time, that I say goodbye to any of my friends." Angie is starting to regret her choice of words, and she asks Michelle what her plans are.

Michelle answers, "I'm staying right here, and we're going to have a sleepover like we used to do."

Angie digs a pillow out from the closet, and wonders if this is a suicide watch. "No, it's not a suicide watch, we believe you," Michelle says laying down and looking up at the glowing stars.

Angie points to Walt's constellation of stars, "Bad cat."

That's the name she gave it now.

"Do you remember when we first met? I'll cherish it forever. I was in the school hallway talking with Doug and Walt, just as lunch was ending. Walt stopped you as you were coming in the door and introduced us. You nodded your head and continued walking. Man, you were such a snob. I can't believe we're even friends now," Michelle says fluffing her pillow. Angie reasons she had to get to class and didn't want to be late, especially on her first day at Hazelton Secondary. "I'm just bugging you. At your memorial when I'm old and grey, sitting with my five grandkids, I'll tell the story of how we really first met." Angie wonders how long that will be from now, being old. Before she can ask Michelle a question, she notices her friend is already asleep. The clock now reads 2:32 in the morning.

Funeral

The clock reads ten in the morning, and her mom knocks on the door politely to get her up. Angie looks around, and Michelle has already gone across the street to have breakfast with her grandmother. After showering and getting dressed, she sits down at the table, eating breakfast. Just as she puts a piece of bacon in her mouth both her parents start talking concurrently. They apologize for everything that happened, and are sorry for the out-of-hand drinking that kept her up at night with the incessant arguing. That they regret stranding her in a village where she had nowhere to go leading her to that night on the overpass. Angie sits there, dumbfounded and confused at this unscheduled bit of honesty. She can only reaffirm she's okay, really, that things are mostly better for everyone now. The two parents hug their daughter before declaring they need to go make final arrangements. Angie's father will meet with Walt's father as they oversee the digging of the grave and making sure the site isn't tampered with. She eats toast while watching a morning game-show. It's when she goes to find jam in the fridge she notices the knives are gone. The pain medicine in the spice cabinet is missing. She checks to see the sleeping pills in the bathroom are also absent. She has no intentions of ending her life, and will not draw attention to the preventative measures they've taken while she was asleep.

The black pants and button-up shirt feel more comfortable than the airy dress Angie wore the night before. Everyone is upstairs when she arrives at Walt's house before the funeral begins. Michelle teases Angie, saying she's a loud snorer like her mom, and she counters that by saying at least she doesn't fart like Michelle does. Angie notices Peter shoveling the snow outside and putting salt in the driveway, ensuring nobody slips or falls when they take the casket out for the last time. She joins him as he finishes up and offers him a coffee. Angie asks what he's going to do when all of this is over, and he explains the daily routine managing the community hall: setting up for bingo, cleaning it up for the elementary students to use in the daytime, and sitting in the concession when they have sports or native dancing practices. Angie, clarifies her question, and asks what is he going to do with his life beyond the daily job? Peter stands there, unsure. He honestly would love to pursue working on art: honing the skills his uncles have been teaching him, becoming better at carving native art, painting, and working on his own pieces. "You'll be famous one day, Peter. Me, I can only draw stick figure cats with smiley faces in my textbooks," she says, hugging him and thanking him for all the help he has done for the family the past week.

Everyone sits in the living room quietly listening to Walt's father speaking to all the family and close friends who have gathered. He thanks them for being there the whole week. Gilbert introduces one of Walt's uncles to say a prayer before leaving one more time. When it is over, the women gather up the wreaths, the flowers, and the foam crosses given to the family. Walt's mom cries when the pallbearers lift the casket off the stand and carefully bring it outside to put into the truck, and everyone follows up to the hall. The hall has not changed, and the floor and aisles have been cleaned of trash or dropped Memorial program pamphlets. The casket is laid on the metal stand, and the ladies place the wreaths and flowers. They all sit down in the chairs awaiting the beginning of the sermon. Some people are crying, others are trying to hold in their tears, and Angie can't believe she is sitting there at that very moment. She stares at the coffin, trying to will Walt back to life with her mind, talking to him in her head, "Wake up, wake up please. It's not too late."

The sermon ends, and the casket is escorted outside by everyone. It is placed in the truck for the trip to the graveyard, each pallbearer holding on tightly to the box. This time, the procession is more personal, and everyone follows the truck on foot as the body is brought to the graveyard. Walt's parents, sister, niece, grandmother, aunts, and uncles walk slowly behind the truck. Angie is walking behind them alongside her parents, with Michelle keeping her company. Angie can feel the snow crunching underneath her boots, and once in a while she steps on a rock the sand truck sprinkled over the road earlier in the morning. The procession walks past Walt's house. "Wake up, we're past your house. You can just get up now, and we'll play pool downstairs like we used to on the weekends," she pleads in her head with tears streaming down her cheeks. They walk past the fire hall where the seven sirens rang a week before. The worn-out log house with the aluminum roof sits there alone, Angie remembers hanging out there with Walt and Michelle talking about UFO's and aliens. "Wake up, your grandmother can make you a hot bowl of baked salmon and potatoes, or even moose stew," Angie thinks. Her tears have stopped for now. The drive straight down the main road past the church and health station is slower. The driver is conscious of not wanting people to feel rushed and accidentally slip on the steep, downward-slanted road. The procession turns left and begins the march to the graveyard straight ahead. When they've passed Angie's house she has stopped her fruitless pleading—there's nothing stopping this procession, and there never was. All that remains is the heartbreak of never seeing her favorite person again.

Standing around the empty hole in the ground Angie looks downward at the cleanly dug grave, inspecting it to see that nobody did anything untoward intending to cast black magic on anyone. Angie holds on tightly to her mom and Michelle's hand as the men lower the coffin into the ground. She cannot help it as she breaks down crying and can only mutter, "Mom," as she turns into her mother's arms to hide her face away from everyone. When she opens her eyes Angie sees everyone in tears, even her dad and Walt's father. Family members are given a red rose, and they line up to say one more goodbye. It feels like it takes Angie so long to outstretch her hand and lightly drop the rose onto the coffin. "Bye, Walt." It makes a small impact noise on the wood. Angie joins the family that has huddled to the side of the main group and hugs everyone hard. The family regained composure just briefly, only to lose it when they start shoveling dirt into the hole.

Uncles pull up with vans to take the family home, not

grimly watch the hole get filled. It's a quiet ride up to the house, it is empty. Everyone sitting on the couch is stunned. Walt's grandmother comforts her daughter. Stephanie tries to entertain Denise on her lap. Walt's father goes outside for a smoke. And Angie is fixated on the empty space where the coffin used to rest. Her throat is sore from crying. In the kitchen, one of Walt's aunts is tending to the pots of soup that are being prepared for the feast, making clam chowder with plenty of vegetables. Elsewhere in the village others are tending to their pots of soup too. Angie hungrily grabs a wrapped fish sandwich from the table platter—for the first time this week she found one that actually has onions in it.

Angie has hidden away from everyone in Stephanie's room. She stands looking out the window at people loading up the truck with everything that was purchased during the long week. They put in the racks of bread, the assorted fruits, and baskets Stephanie and Nadine assembled. When Gilbert's truck is full, Angie's dad pulls up and they load that truck. Walt's mom enters the room standing next to Angie and gives her a golden-brown piece of fried bread. It is so soft, chewy, and when she takes a bite she savors the butter on top. "I believe what you said last night, Angie. You will live a long life, wherever it takes you, and Walt will watch over you like he always did. I'm not worried the way other people are—you won't do what you were considering doing. That's in the past. You're our family, and we will always love you," Walt's mom says before going to the kitchen to check on the soup. Denise comes stomping in barefoot and reaching for the fried bread. Angie sits with her as they share it on the bed.

"Just wait until we take you to Terrace or Hazelton, we'll order you a big plate of fried rice, chow mein, and dry garlic spareribs like your uncle. But first, you will need to grow your teeth," Angie promises Denise as they look down in the back-yard at trucks being filled up with feast supplies.

Feast

The Gitksan people have practiced holding Feasts for countless generations and hundreds of years. Even during the era of assimilation when laws were enacted to stop this tradition, this system has endured through time. The young are encouraged to attend feasts, to participate and observe what happens in the Feast hall, and then teach the next generation to keep the culture alive. Not all feasts are the same, and what happens tonight in the hall may differ from what would happen in other communities up and down the Skeena River. There is no textbook guide or instruction manual on how communities carry out feasts, but there are sacred laws that need to be observed as a sign of respect to the grieving family hosting tonight's Feast and to the honored guests who'll be in attendance. Tonight is the Settlement Feast where debts are paid, thanks are given, and everything is observed publicly by the witnesses in attendance.

It begins with unloading everything that has been bought, cooked, and bundled together during the week. The Feast is hosted by the mother's side of the deceased. In an organized fashion, the whole racks of bread, bulk boxes of soup crackers, and assorted fruits are stored in the back of the Feast hall to be handed out later in the evening for the guests. Each table in the Feast hall has been set up with cutlery, napkins, and mini paper plates with sugar packets for people's coffee. Coffee is freshly made in large metal percolators that are kept in the community hall for such events and gatherings. Each member of the immediate family from the maternal side is expected to bring a pot of soup to the hall or, when necessary, hire someone trusted to make a pot of soup if the family is busy. When making soup for feasts most people go with the standard selection of clam chowder, steak soup, or seafood soup as the primary course to be served at the Feast. The pots of soup are kept warm on the community hall stove and on the hotplates that were borrowed for such occasions. The pots of soup will be brought out after the Feast has started after the guests have arrived and introductory speeches are made. When the hall is at full capacity, meeting local fire safety standards, it is expected to be filled with over three hundred people as they arrive at 6:00pm, the time set by the family when it was announced at the Smoke Feast earlier in the week. After unloading everything, ensuring the soup is being kept warm and all the tables are ready, the host clan waits for the guests to arrive.

People arrive and line up at the entrance of the hall. They are escorted to their respective tables based on which house clan they belong to. If they are a Hereditary Chief, a *Simogyet*, they sit at the head table in the front of the hall as is the custom. Each major clan in the community has its own row of tables that spans the length of the hall, and there is a special guest table set for visiting members that don't belong to the major houses. Before being shown to the seat, if an arriving guest holds a Gitksan name it is announced, indicating they are in attendance of the Feast. When all the guests have arrived, and are properly seated, the Feast is formally started with a prayer, and the food and offerings are blessed.

It pains Angie that she can't help Walt's family for the evening. She wishes she was at the back of the hall, tearing open the fruit boxes and teaming up with someone to hand them out to the guests. Angie is not of the Grouse and Fireweed Clan, the *Gisghast*. She belongs to the same house as her mother, the Wolf Clan, the *Laxgibuu*. She can only watch alongside her mother, with Michelle, also from the *Laxgibuu* Clan, sitting opposite her on the same table next to her grandmother. Angie nods to her father sitting one row over, he belongs to the Frog Clan, *Ganada*, and next to her father sits Walt's father, who can't serve, either. As was the custom in the past the Frog Clan sits on the western side of the hall where the sun sets. If the Grouse Clan wasn't serving tonight, they would be seated on the eastern side of the hall where the sun rises. In the middle of the hall are the tables for the Wolf, Eagle (*Laxw Skeek*), and Visitors tables.

The Feast has officially begun when the pots of hot soup are brought to the front of each clan's table. Members from the Grouse Clan will serve the soup to each guest, ensuring throughout the night their bowls will never be empty. Stephanie and Walt's cousin, Eric, work as a team on the Wolf Clan table. Eric takes the glass bowl Angie brought with her from home to fill it up with soup, then returns it to her. Not long after, Eric's mom, also serving, drops off a full packet of crackers to go with her soup. Each person sitting at the table gets one full log of crackers, more than they will need. But it is the custom in the Feast hall to treat every guest generously. The soup is still hot and delicious as Angie and Michelle enjoy what they were given; it wasn't the clam chowder soup Walt's mother spent the day preparing, but instead a seafood soup filled with salmon chunks, sea weed, and crab meat. Angie recognizes the work; Walt's grandmother made the soup and went all out providing a healthy mixture of ingredients to savor. Stephanie and Eric return, handing out loaves of bread to each person sitting on the Wolf Clan table. Michelle smiles at Eric—he recognizes her from the gas station and as the teacher's assistant from school; he is about to hand her a loaf of bread from Angie's side of the table. Stephanie lets out a corrective cough and Eric stops. Eric is reminded that it's disrespectful to reach across a Feast table to hand out items. He should only serve items on his side of the table. He doesn't want to spill people's tea, coffee, soda, or soup. If a guest has their soup or drinks spilled, or has something spilled on them by the host clan, they will need to be properly compensated and the compensation publicly paid out in front of the Feast hall guests—an apology from the host clan for everyone to see. Angie remembers learning that lesson when she had to serve at her grandmother's Feast. Not that she had an accident, but she was scolded by her mom for trying to cheat too.

Michelle is the first to finish the soup she was originally given. Before she can turn her bowl over, signifying she is full and doesn't want to be served anymore soup, Eric scoops the plate from her and returns with another hot bowl of seafood soup. The servers next begin handing out the fruits Angie helped buy earlier in the week. Next to her soup bowl she sees bananas, apples, and oranges. As is the custom with the Feast, when everyone has been served, the remaining items are brought to the Chiefs sitting at the head table. Angie can see Eric nodding dutifully to each Chief as he hands them the remaining box of apples. Serving in a Feast is very hectic. When Angie served it felt like a marathon relay of taking food boxes, distributing it to the guests, and grabbing a new box to start all over or having to do patrols on the assigned table refilling soup bowls. Angie's mom stops Stephanie as she returns from the Chiefs' table. She asks if she can call dibs on one of the now empty boxes that used to hold the apples. Angie's mom will use this box to carry home the excess bread, fruits, and crackers for her and her daughter when the Feast is over. For now, she will tuck it under the table out of sight. Stephanie, now perspiring visibly, is called to hand each guest soda and ask each guest if they want regular or diet, which was provided for those with health issues such as diabetes.

Sitting at the Feast table is a communal experience where people can socialize with one another. Angie and Michelle talk with an older couple from out of town about their plans for schooling and careers. Angie's mom catches up with old high school friends she doesn't have time to see normally. Peter and Doug stop by the table for a brief chat before returning to their tables. At the back of the hall Angie can see Stephanie laughing and joking with distant family. Even though the Feast is a result of immeasurable loss, people in attendance put the crippling grief aside to greet those they haven't seen in a long time.

The word *Hawal* is incredibly important in Gitksan culture. Plainly put it means to "Put Into The Pot." In other villages and communities a copper plate would be used where people would drop off their monetary contribution. Instead, a carved and wooden painted box is used this evening. Money dropped into the box will help the family cover accrued expenses from the death of the clan member. Most of the money goes directly to paying for the casket and work done at the Smithers funeral home. As the serving of food winds down, a line of Chiefs from the Grouse Clan forms near the microphone at the entrance of the hall next to the painted wooden box, to contribute their portion to help cover funeral-related expenses. It starts with the head Chiefs—they contribute the most as they hand over money put into the carving box. When they contribute, they tell the person at the microphone their Gitksan name and how much they contributed. The person accepting the money repeats this as he puts the money into the box, a public receipt of the *Hawal.* As the line progresses the amounts given get smaller. It is against custom to give more than the Chief in the Feast hall. When the end of the line nears there are those from the Grouse Clan without a Chief or Gitksan name. Their amount is lowest, and instead they say their legal name. Eric doesn't hold a Gitksan name, not yet, but he is happy when the man holding the microphone says his full name and the dollar amount he gave to help his house Clan.

To hold a Gitksan name carries benefits and responsibilities. Hereditary Chiefs are responsible for teaching and enforcing ancient Gitksan Laws and Traditions within their Houses. As a member of the Gitksan tribe participates in the culture, at certain points in their life they may attain a name or inherit a new name. A Gitksan name grants one rights to use portions of Gitksan land to hunt, fish, or gather firewood for basic survival through the year. The higher the name a person holds, the more they are expected to contribute during feasts. The Hereditary Chiefs with the biggest names are the ones that pay the most when it is their time to contribute and give their *Hawal* when a member of their clan dies. Walt never had a Gitksan name, neither does Angie. If he did, the feast process would be different as someone from the Grouse Clan would have inherited his name and be bound to certain obligations, namely be required to pay for the fence and headstone within a year of his death. In this instance, the mother's clan will collectively raise funds for the fence and pay for the headstone to be installed on top of the grave. This is not covered by the *Hawal*, this is a long-standing tradition for those inheriting a Gitksan or Chief name, to fulfill the obligation to the deceased.

After the *Hawal* is given the family has a brief huddle with the MC at the microphone. He announces who will do the counting. Angie's mother isn't surprised when her name is called out, alongside that of Doug's father. They have been entrusted with counting and documenting the total sum of money given to the pot. Angie's mom knew she would be called up and had the foresight to bring paper, pens, and a calculator. She finishes the last of her bowl of soup and turns it over.

The counting of the money is now underway. During this time, Walt's mother, sister, and assorted aunts and uncles go to a side room in the hall to retrieve the gift baskets assembled. Each basket or large plastic tote is a thank you to those who served critical roles aiding the family when they needed it the most, who weren't bound by Clan obligations. Angie helped put together those totes, labeled the names with freezer tape and a marker, and ensured everything intended to be given was accounted for. The mother Clan brings every tote to the floor next to the table where the *Hawal* is being counted. They are lined up in chronological order. Walt's mother isn't much of a public speaker, even though she holds a high-standing Gitksan name within her *Wilp* (house). She starts by thanking everyone for coming to the Feast. She confesses how hard the week has been dealing with the loss of her son, but how she is glad to have so many people help carry the family through the past week and a half. The first name called out is that of Walt's godfather—he drove the casket home in his truck, leading the procession of cars from Smithers to Gitsegukla. Stephanie strains as she picks up the basket and walks towards the Eagle Clan table. She puts the basket beside him; he thanks her for the gift and offers his deepest condolences. While Walt's mom and Stephanie keep a clean house there was no way they'd be able to keep up with cleaning during the week it was filled with visitors. A homemaker was tasked to help clean the house from the day before the Smoke Feast to the day of the funeral. Walt's aunt picks up the basket to drop it off at the table of the Homemaker for all the hard work she did during the past week. When news broke of the death the family knew the narrow stairway and tight turn at the top of the staircase would not fit the casket when the body was brought home. It was decided that the village's local carpenters would need to build an external staircase leading up to the patio, and that they would have to use the balcony sliding glass door to bring the body in and out of the house. Each of the carpenters that built that stairway are named and their baskets are delivered. Inside is a collection of usable everyday items such as towels, drinking glasses, and—in the case of the carpenters—new tools and electric drills. Walt's uncles who served as the night watchmen are then thanked for the hours spent guarding the house and patrolling the yard ensuring nobody would tamper with the casket; they, too, receive a large tote of goods to bring home after the Feast has finished. Walt's mom then lists all the bookkeeping and accounting Angie's mom did during the week, helping Stephanie document and record who did what. She thanks her for driving them to the airport when they went to pick up Walt's body. She hugs Angie's mom and personally presents her with a basket; the basket is then delivered to Angie at her table. The last two baskets are given to Doug's father and Angie's father for digging the grave, and Stephanie and Eric's mom deliver those baskets last. Walt's mother thanks everyone for coming to the Feast. She thanks everyone who helped the family during the hard week of grieving and finishes her speech, relieved that this major portion of the Feast process is now completed.

People finish eating the last of their soup bowls and flip them over. They wait patiently as the money is counted. Walt's mom gets up from the back of the hall, from sitting with the rest of her Clan, to join the huddle at the table when the counting is completed. The Chief of the host Clan is holding a piece of paper and announces the sum of all the *Hawal* given by the Clan. Then the Chief of the Clan reads out how much will be paid out to cover the funeral-related costs: the amount for the coffin, the travel expenses required to bring the body from Toronto, the clothing expenses for the suit, and wages of those who helped during the week. Within each basket handed out in thanks is also an envelope containing a fair payment for services rendered.

When Angie was younger and spent Sunday mornings visiting her then-still-living grandparents in the house they since inherited, they would tell her stories about the old days. Stories of the government officials and local police trying to shut down Feasts when they would happen. Feasts would have to be held in secret to avoid interference. She later learned that this was in part because of the Red Scare, as the former Soviet Union rose in stature after World War Two. There's an event that happens in the Feast hall that was regarded as communistic in nature. First Nations, at the time, had no interest in communism or any other ideology, they were only interested in practicing their culture and heritage. The word for what happens next is *Gwiikw*. Hunters in the village recognize the word as Groundhog, but in the Feast hall context the word means "Buy" or "Purchase." It is a final thank you to the guests who witnessed the Feast proceedings. Angie's mom and her assistant have finished counting the money. The Chief of the Grouse Clan reads to the hall how much was raised, and exactly how much was paid out. Most Feasts raise enough to cover funeral-related expenses. When a Chief or significant member of the community passes, there's always some left over after everything is paid out. The left over money is distributed to all the seated guests in the hall, the amount based on their stature within the Gitksan community.

Several individuals from the Grouse Clan, the hosting Clan, are selected for their intimate knowledge of everyone in attendance at the Feast. These individuals know who is who in the Feast hall, their stature if they hold a Gitksan name, or those who don't yet hold Gitksan names. Stephanie is one of the few folk selected to hand out the *Gwiikw*, one last thank you to those who attended the Feast. She, along with several others, are entrusted with distributing the unused *Hawal* to the people sitting at the tables. The Chiefs at the head table at the front of the hall get the largest sum when the *Gwiikw* is handed out as respect for their stature in the community. Others in the hall receive less in proportion to the name they hold. When Stephanie arrives at Angie's table she politely leaves the bare minimum that is given out to those who don't hold a Gitksan name. Angie has received a small amount as someone without a Gitksan name. Across the table, Michelle, who has a small Gitksan name as a member of the Wolf Clan, has received slightly more than Angie.

To attend a Feast means to sit in the hall from the opening prayer to the closing prayer. It is absolutely disrespectful to the Gitksan people, and to the Clan hosting the Feast, to get up and leave at any time. It is especially shameful if someone were to pack up their bowls, accumulated bread, fruit, and crackers and leave immediately after receiving the *Gwiikw*. People don't think anybody notices when that is done, but everyone notices and it sets a bad example to the young who are learning Feast hall traditions. It has become a problem at times where Chiefs from all the houses have to publicly remind their Clan members that leaving a Feast hall is not allowed unless there's a family emergency. And if someone has to leave the hall, they need to publicly address the host Clan before leaving, explaining why they have to go. This is why the host Clan sits at the entrance of the hall where the counting table is located, and the microphone is situated. It would be obvious to see someone leaving early. The same applies for the Chief table at the back of the hall. They sit, observing at the head table next to both the rear fire exits, mindful of the actions of those who would leave through the back door. Angie looks around after the *Gwiikw* is handed out to everyone. She is thankful the tables are full and nobody is making a beeline for the exits.

Walt's mother, sister, and grandmother assembled a list of every Chief holding a significant Gitksan name in attendance of the Feast. At various points in the night, they privately confirm they'd be willing to make a speech from their respective House Clans before the closing prayer is said. Stephanie travels around the hall with the list and a cordless microphone in hand. She walks to the first Chief on their list, a Chief who is one of Angie's distant uncles from her mother's side of the family. "Simgiget, Sigidimhaahanak, ganhl k'uba wilksasxw." Translated means, "Gentlemen, ladies, and the little ones." Every speaker uses this opening. He speaks loudly and clearly; he has prepared what he intended to say to Walt's clan who are hosting the Feast. His words are spoken in the Gitksan language. It is frowned upon to speak in English when addressing the Feast hall, as this is aimed to encourage every parent and family to teach the language to the young and that they shouldn't cheat and have the words translated to English. Angie is at a disadvantage as she sits there trying to make out the fluent Gitksan phrasing being used. She can only pick apart a few words here and there. Her family raised her in Vancouver as a child, and she didn't have the opportunity to speak Gitksan in her house or practice with her extended family. Now she's playing catch up being taught by her mom, Michelle, Michelle's grandmother, and Walt's parents. Every person who speaks offers their condolences to Walt's parents and family, to his clan for such a sudden unexpected loss. Some deliver speeches about how happy they are seeing so many young children and teenagers learning the ways of the Feast hall and that nobody left after the *Gwiikw*. Walt's family listens to these words as the trying week comes to a close.

At the end, a prayer is given, thanking those who've cooked the soup, the bread, and a wish is made for everyone to get home safely. Words are spoken, hoping it will be a long time before another Feast will be hosted in the community, in the hall, that death takes a break from visiting Gitsegukla. Everyone then packs up the bowls and utensils they brought, and some who planned ahead put their bread, crackers, and fruits into plastic or canvas tote bags. While some exit through the rear fire exits, most people make an effort to leave through the front entrance and shake the hand of Walt's family as they depart, offering their sympathy or a long hug. Everyone has left the Feast hall in an orderly fashion. They now warm up their cars or trucks to defrost the windows. Angie and Michelle stand with Walt's family looking out at the empty Feast hall. None of them say anything as they walk out the door, but they all know it is over and each of them still hurt from their loss.

The Burning

Angie opens her eyes at 10:23am to the sound of her bedroom door creaking. She looks outside through the window and the sky is cloudy hinting it will probably snow. The Feast did not finish until 1:30 in the morning, and then she left the hall and returned home with her parents. She can hear someone cooking food in the kitchen. Things feel so different now—yesterday happened, and it is all so final. Angie didn't get to bed until three. She still wishes she could bring him back to life or go back in time to save him, but she doesn't have super powers or some elaborate time travel machine, and she realizes she should know better than to obsess over fantasies that will never come true. She doesn't know what happens next, school? The union is still on strike, and negotiations are coming along slowly. It's not like she can load up her car and drive to Prince George. Michelle's boss wouldn't appreciate Angie hanging around all day and only allowed it during the past week while the family was grieving. For now, she decided she'll babysit Denise for free if Stephanie ever needs to go do her own thing or when the family hosts the next bingo. The VHF radio seems lively now as people have their usual conversations publicly over the air, people asking if they've seen their kids and wanting them sent home. During the week when the body was present most people avoided using the radio out of respect for the family. Angie can hear two old ladies talking about what snacks they're giving their kids for a swimming field trip the next day.

Angie gets up and stands on her bed, looking out the window. She can see Michelle carrying chopped firewood into the basement. She looks left at the narrow road leading to the graveyard. Angie wonders if it is too soon to visit his grave?

Watching the afternoon news, eating a late breakfast, Angie sits quietly with her parents. There is still no update or progress with the teacher's strike. Drivers had a bad morning with the new snowfall around Vancouver, and the hockey team won the night before. Angie's dad waits for a commercial break before telling them he is leaving for Vancouver the next day. Without thinking, she just asks, "Why?" She realizes he has to go back to work, and that he has a family waiting for him, but it feels too soon to leave everyone like this. He asks her if she wants to come visit since the school is still on strike. Angie's father leaves and walks down the narrow road to perform one last check on the grave, making sure nothing is out of place. Angie's mother works on her laptop at the kitchen table, so she turns the television off and goes back to her bedroom. Reading up on emails she sees nothing noteworthy, just junk ads and phishing scams. Angie takes the black dress she wore from the door hanger and puts it in her closet, wrapping it in plastic until it is needed next time, but before she does she removes the black and white ribbon that was given to her at the Memorial. Everyone from the family will wear that until they are no longer in a period of grieving. She transfers the ribbon to the left arm of her black winter coat. While she lies on her bed looking at photos of Walt on her phone the doorbell rings, she goes to answer it, Karen stops to say goodbye before going back to school in Edmonton. Like Walt's school, they aren't affected by the ongoing strike. The two promise to keep in touch and call should either of them want to talk or comfort one another. Michelle walks across the street as Karen drives away, and she asks if Angie wants to go pick up burgers and fries in town. Angie wants to stay inside for the day, she doesn't want to go right back to things being normal, and explains she might go visit Walt's family.

Angie hasn't driven her car in a week and a half. It took a while for it to warm up, and she fought to clean off the hardened snow and frost from the windows. When she arrives up at his house she finds that Walt's dad and sister are just finishing restoring the living room to its original state. The coffee table is back near the main couch. The second couch is brought upstairs from the basement. The television is back in the corner, with Denise enjoying children's cartoons and drinking from a juice box. Denise gets bored with the television and comes back from the bedroom with a bag full of blocks and dumps them on the floor. She plays in the dining room area, occasionally trying to get her mom to see her stacking them as high as she can. Walt's dad has changed the channel to the afternoon hockey game. Angie sits next to Stephanie at the kitchen table, reading the newspaper. Denise can be heard stacking the blocks and giggling when she knocks them over. Stephanie gently reminds her to not be so rough or throw the blocks too far. Angie goes to the kitchen to pour herself a cup of tea. She notices the serving trays that used to hold sandwiches and cookies have been returned to their original owners. And the giant coffee maker is also gone too. She stands near the sink, stirring sugar into her cup of tea. From the corner of her eye she can see Denise has made a pyramid-shaped stack at her mom's feet. Angie turns her head to put the lid back onto the sugar bowl. In her peripheral vision she sees Denise about to put the final block up, but the pyramid falls over. Denise laughs again, amused, and kicks the rest of the blocks away with her feet. Angie just realized she must have been seeing things, she only kicked them away with her short little feet, the blocks weren't falling over on their own. Everyone finds a spot on the couches quietly watching the game after Angie's dad arrives. During the commercial break he tells them the grave looks fine and nothing is out of place. Walt's mom went down to his grand-mother's place to visit for the afternoon. She phoned up, ask-ing Stephanie to take meat out of the freezer so she can make it for dinner. Denise tries to be patient sitting on Angie's lap, but gets cranky. Angie takes her to the bedroom, and they lay down reading a storybook about lions and tigers.

When she wakes up from an unexpected nap she sees De-nise still sleeping next to her. Walt's father and sister have already gone up to the gym to help fundraise for an elder needing assistance for a medical trip the next week. Walt's mom greets Angie as she walks into the living room. Nadine tells her there's a nice hot plate of moose stew on the stove waiting for her and reminds her where she can find the cur-ry. While quietly enjoying the rice and gravy she stares at his mother, wondering how is she doing. Is she being strong like Angie is trying to be, but barely keeping it together? Walt's mother relates how sad his grandmother is at the moment, that she didn't even want to go to bingo when Nadine of-fered to pay for her cards. Everyone is trying to adjust to the change today, but things are off. Angie asks how Nadine cut her finger; she got a tiny slice when she was picking up bro-ken glass. When Nadine was visiting she didn't put her coffee mug on the table properly, and it fell off the edge onto the floor. Angie pulls out the backseat picture of her and Walt and sits next to his mom, asking about it. Stephanie isn't in the picture because she wanted to go berry picking with her grandparents, and she cried violently because she didn't want to go to Vancouver for that trip. The idea flashes into Angie's mind of taking Denise to the aquarium next summer, maybe introducing Denise to Angie's brother.

After the late dinner Walt's mom goes to sleep in her bed-room. Angie entertains Denise after she wakes up from her sleep. Outside the window she can hear the kids laughing as they slide down the hill again. It's not long before she sees Michelle racing past, heading up the hill on her snowmobile. Angie feels bad that she refused Michelle's offer of burgers and a chance to go visit Peter who had rented movies for the night. But she promised she would babysit for the evening. The bingo ends, and Stephanie and her dad return home; they are happy they raised enough for the elder's medical trip. De-nise runs to greet her mom, knowing they have bingo pop for her. Angie drives down to her house after everyone has settled. On the way down, she sees that Walt's grandmother's lights are all off. When she gets out of her car she notices the dogs aren't howling anymore. The street is still and quiet. She enters her own house and joins her parents in the living room once more. Her dad asks when they'll be doing the burning. It takes Angie a while to figure out the question and realizes *the burning*. Stephanie and Walt's mom will decide the time to do that next. They still have to go through his belongings and sort out Walt's possessions. When they've assembled what clothes or items he'll need on the other side, the belongings will be burned, similar to how they give him food by putting it in the fire. Angie wonders how that works with modern items. They can't just throw computers, phones, or toxic plastics in the fire. Angie remembers they did the same when her grandmother died, that her mom sorted and found her grandmother's favorite clothes and put them into the fire days after the funeral. Angie's dad falls asleep on the couch after the news broadcast has finished, so she turns off the television before going to her room. Even though she took a long nap she doesn't want to ruin her sleeping pattern and forces herself to lay in bed. She looks up at the fake, glowing stars, and then hears a faint noise of fabric and plastic sliding in her closet. Turning on the lights and opening the closet door she sees the black funeral dress has fallen to the floor. She puts it back on the hanger, and then forces herself to sleep.

The next morning Angie stands in the cold wind, hugging her dad bye and wishing him a safe trip back south. She promises she will visit next summer and hopes he will bring his family back up for a Christmas visit, but he makes no promises. After Angie's mother goes to work Michelle stops by to catch up before she goes to work too. Angie ponders finding a job while the strike continues on—it would help to have money for the Christmas list she's been forming in her head.

Michelle is happy to have Angie home. She has already made plans for the both of them, to hang out at the mall, sit on the bench, and play their gambling numbers. Maybe go to the bar and go dancing. Angie senses Michelle is trying to get around to saying something—there's an elusiveness to their conversation that makes Angie think she wants to bring something up. Michelle doesn't have to play any further games and just blurts it out, "We had a haunting happen yesterday."

Angie replies, "Haunting?"

Michelle explains that a spirit or ghost of someone is upset or unsettled. That sometimes it's a bowl getting knocked off a table, kitchen cabinet doors opening or closing, doors slamming shut, or creaking noises in the night. The more serious hauntings are scarier, such as echoes of children laughing or old ladies crying, dark shadows in the corner of peoples' eyes following them around their house. Michelle explains that last night her bedroom door slowly squeaked open and she could hear footsteps walking away down the hall.

"Is this bad? Is something evil happening?" Angie asks as she recalls the last scary ghost-demon movie she watched.

Michelle reassures her that Walt's spirit hasn't gone evil or vengeful, that this process isn't complete just yet, that the family has done the Feast, they thanked all who helped the family, and next his belongings need to be delivered to the other side. Angie is skeptical of all of this, but Michelle believes it is true. Angie has doubts as she puts together the instances of the broken coffee mug of Walt's mom, the blocks Denise was playing with being knocked over, and her own dress sliding off the hanger the night before.

"If you can talk with his parents about doing the burning, it will settle him. Don't be scared, Angie, it's just how it is." Michelle says.

The family finds themselves in the backyard belonging to Walt's grandmother the next day. It seems everyone in the immediate family had some unexplainable phenomenon occur that accelerated the schedule of the planned burning. This special place is the same spot where they burned the items of Walt's grandfather when he died. Walt's father has finished lighting the fire in the secluded pit near the cellar where the family stores the year's harvested potatoes. Walt's grandmother stands next to his mother, both shivering in the cold. His little cousin Eric is next to Angie, quiet. Stephanie and her dad bring out the boxes she sorted the night before. Walt's mother cries when the boxes are put down near the fire, as this is one last final goodbye. They witness the burning of the last connection Walt has to this world, delivering the items he will need going forward. Walt's mother starts with the box of clothes. Angie recognizes his favorite blue, stripped, button-up shirt—it goes into the fire, and the dark blue jeans he always wore go into the fire. His favorite hockey jersey is next put into the fire. Angie remembers standing outside the Vancouver hockey arena, waiting because he wanted to have his jersey signed, but that never happened. Next his favorite shoes and boots are put into the fire. Stephanie joins her mother in putting clothes into the fire. Everyone stands there watching the items burn, some crying. Angie reaches into the box and takes out some of his favorite books. She hopes he will enjoy reading them again when he gets them, then tosses them into the fire. The fire heats up as all the items are burned, a few people drive slowly past, watching the family perform this last act.

Next, Walt's uncle prepares a plate of burning sweet grass. Not all of Walt's belongings can be burned, so instead they will be passed on as mementos in his memory. Eric is called up first, and he is handed a box, then he looks down into it. The smoke of the sweet grass is wafted around Eric and the box. It has been blessed and ownership of the video game system and games has passed on to Walt's little cousin. Walt's laptop and computer are bathed in the smoke and are passed on to Stephanie and Denise. Gilbert goes to the truck and struggles as he brings out the next item, then he solemnly hands it to Angie who nods as she accepts it. Walt's uncle washes Angie in the smoke of the sweet grass and the giant telescope she holds in her hands. Everyone is given an item, and each takes a moment thinking about him, before they all go inside where Walt's grandmother made baked salmon and boiled potatoes for dinner. In the kitchen, Angie listens to Walt's mother talk with her sisters about the disturbances people have been sharing with her in private. Walt's mother hopes it's all over with, that her son will now rest in peace.

After the dinner, Angie sits at the kitchen table while others have moved to the couches. The house is full; it reminds her of last Christmas when Walt dragged her there to visit his side of the family. Once in a while she looks outside as the fire slowly burns out. Michelle slides her finger against the blade, checking to see if they're still sharp. The skates were blessed and passed on to her; it was curious that she has the same foot size as Walt. "I remember that time he played hockey in Hazelton and scored three goals. Three goals!" Michelle puts the skates in the box, planning to go for a skate as soon as she can. Michelle talks with Walt's dad about hunting for rabbits the upcoming weekend. Angie takes the opportunity to stop by and visit Eric who went to his room. She finds him playing the video games he inherited.

"How'd you get so good?" Eric asks as Angie snipes a guy's head clean off.

"Walt would force me to play these games with him when I'd visit up at his house," Angie explains.

It always surprised the guys at her dorm she could handle her own when it came to video games. She found it kind of annoying how some of them would get condescending or even threatened by her gaming skills. She never liked the first-person shooters, though. Playing pool or darts were her favorite games, and even a good pinball table here and there.

When the dinner is over Angie returns home and catches up with her mom. The two stare curiously at the giant, oversized telescope. November is always a cloudy month, the snow building up unrelenting until the deep freeze of January. There's no chance for Angie to take the telescope outside on her back patio for star or moon gazing. Angie hauls the telescope to her room and puts it in the corner. In the middle of logging onto her email at her desk Angie hears the thump. A quiet, gentle thump behind her, something hitting the thick carpet. She doesn't know if she should freak out now. Should she call her mom, or Walt's parents, or have the uncle bless it again? Angie looks down at the telescope that was once propped securely against the corner, and is now on the floor. "What do you want, Walt? What is bothering you out there?" she thinks in her head, hoping he will answer. There is no answer. She looks around the room, waiting for something else to fall down or move unexpectedly. For now, she leaves the telescope on the floor and checks her emails. A few friends from school are asking for updates on how she is doing. A guy she vaguely knows wants to catch up when school resumes. There's a chain letter email from Michelle that she deletes. Just as she's about to log out she sees two messages in her junk mail folder—normally she would let them get automatically erased, but instead she checks them. She has two messages from James. Angie recognizes the email domain name—it's the same university account Walt would send his emails from. "Who are you, James, and why are you contacting me?"

It took him some time, but he finally found her. The school was no help, with no one there to provide any contact information because of the strike, and they wouldn't either to protect her privacy. There were no friends of friends he could get in touch with. All James knew about Angie was that Walt regarded her as an adopted sister the family took in, a great friend he missed in his two years spent at Toronto, and that she was a fan of The Tragically Hip. Walt had sent her a collection of albums and bootleg mix tapes he had found at record stores on Yonge Street. With that to go on, James found her fan blog. In that particular space on the internet he found an email address and hoped she would reply. The first email is similar to the other well wishes and deepest condolences people have been offering the past few weeks. The other email gets her attention, and Angie goes to her mom's room and asks to be driven to the airport the next morning.

She wishes she came here under better circumstances, to surprise Walt when he was still alive. In the distance is the CN Tower by the lake. Angie's first impression of Toronto is how smooth the cab ride is compared to the tiny reserve a day away with the potholes and bumpy roads. The trip was so long that she makes it halfway through the book Michelle loaned her the night before. Michelle wanted to come, but couldn't afford it. The cab drops her off at the corner of St. George Street and Harbord. It's a full block away from her intended destination, as she would later learn. Angie's second impression of Toronto is of the big, weird, turkey-shaped building. A girl passing by explains to Angie that it's a giant turkey-shaped library. It would be criminal if that building didn't hold a thanksgiving dinner inside it. Angie's third impression of Toronto is the wind. Even though Gitsegukla village is surrounded by mountains, at a higher elevation, and is under several feet of snow, the wind is not as bad at home. She walks north one block. The exterior of the dorm building is clean, and she enters the lobby and is greeted by the desk clerk. He makes a few calls on her behalf, and it's barely a few minutes before she meets James. The two say hello and he invites her upstairs. The halls are filled with life—students talking about classes, music can be heard through open doors, and some coming back from late-night study sessions. Angie finds herself missing this, thinking about the empty hallways in Prince George.

James and his girlfriend welcome Angie to the shared dorm Walt used to live in. They all sit on the couch. He explains the other roommates accepted the grief offer and have taken the rest of the semester off, so James and Talia are the only ones there. "I think Sam would have loved to meet you too," Talia says. Angie asks who Sam is. "One of his computer science friends, now grieving back at home in Montreal." The two speak nicely about Walt in the short time they knew him. How quiet he was when they first met, how he kept to himself focusing on school, and was at first afraid to do things with them. He slowly got to know them over the first month, opening up, accepting their invites to go see movies and get pizza down the street. Talia hands Angie a piece of paper. It has contact information of Walt's friends, general email addresses, and phone numbers. James hands Angie a card, a condolences card signed by everyone who was saddened when Walt died. They didn't have an address to send the card to when his parents quickly made arrangements to bring him home.

James leads Angie to the room at the end of the hall. He turns on the light after opening the door and shows her into Walt's old room. There is no trace he once lived there, or died. The bed is new, the desk space cleaned spotless, and the carpet washed. Angie wonders if the next kid who moves in here will be told what happened? Will he think the room is haunted? "Don't worry, imaginary kid I never met, this room won't be haunted," Angie completes the train of thought that popped into her head. Angie looks out the window from the fourth floor, and she imagines him doing the same, seeing the pedestrians down below fighting the howling wind. She sits down on the bed, staring at his desk, at the empty phone jack. On the desk are Walt's glasses. Angie wonders if bringing these home will give him peace. She takes them and puts them in the inside pocket of her jacket. Before leaving, she checks the entire room: underneath the bed, under the desk, in the closet, in the desk drawers, and behind the door. James explains he found the glasses several days after the body was brought home, and after the bed was replaced by the maintenance staff. In the panic of trying to revive him the glasses were knocked under the bed. It was James who called building security to check in on Walt that morning—the two had plans to sneak off to get hockey tickets for their circle of friends. Then everything after that just went to hell. James asks Angie to come get pizza with them, but she has to decline so she can get back to the airport for the flight back home at midnight. Talia runs to James' room and returns, then hands Angie a picture. Seated in the booth at the pizza place a block away is Walt and his roommates the first time they all went out after exams had been taken. Walt looks tired, but happy since he survived his first month in Toronto. Angie remembers the phone call that night. She was studying for her first batch of exams, worried, and Walt comforted her, telling her that she would pass like she always does. The two walk Angie down to the front entrance of the building and quietly wait with her for the cab to pick her up. They hug her before she leaves, expressing their sorrow for the loss.

Angie sits in the waiting area at the airport after checking in, and the space is nearly empty. She takes the time to read the text messages from her mom and Michelle and replies, telling them she's on her way home again. Angie opens the book and reads it, and halfway through the page she feels it. A light, airy breeze that doesn't give her a chill, but it feels like a presence next to her. Angie takes out the glasses from her pocket and looks at them. "Are you with me, Walt? I'm bringing you home now." She doesn't know what will happen with the glasses when she gets back, if they would get burned, or blessed with smoke, or left in his bedroom. Angie remembers the hurt of getting her first pair of glasses, being teased, getting called a nerd and a geek. Walt never had that problem when he got his glasses. He was just himself and wasn't insecure about who he was. Most people liked him enough to not make a big deal when he got them when he started grade eleven. Angie puts the glasses back in the pocket and then stares at the photo she was given. The plane boards and flies away to the West. Angie watches the lights of Toronto get dimmer, thankful the seat next to her is empty.

The descent into Vancouver wakes her up from the dream she had about a hike, a surreal trek into a lush, green forest. Angie wipes the drool off her chin before getting off the plane. She rushes to get breakfast before the connecting flight to Smithers. Angie stops at the gift shop to pick Denise up a hockey jersey, with the same team and player Walt once owned before it was burned. She doesn't really know why; Stephanie isn't a big hockey fan, and Denise is too young to have an appreciation or allegiance to a team. Two hours later she finally arrives in Smithers and is greeted by Walt's sister. Stephanie asks about his roommate, James. Angie hands her the condolence card as they walk to the truck. It's a quiet ride to the village, and Angie is happy to see the familiar mountain ranges again. The ride reminds her of the procession leading to the Smoke Feast a week and a half before. There isn't a line of thirty-three cars behind them this time.

The village shows signs of life as they pull in. People are out going to the mailbox to check their mail. Some folk have started the draining task of shoveling snow that fell overnight, and the community maintenance crew are plowing and sanding the roads. Angie feels the recognizable bumps in the road as they drive up to Walt's house, and she waves at Peter as he walks down the overpass. Pulling into the driveway, Walt's mom can be seen in the window looking out at them. She picks up Denise and makes her wave to her mom. Walt's dad is waiting for Angie at the top of the stairs, and she sees him holding the key in his hand. When she gets to the top of the stairs he unlocks the padlock and opens the door to the room. Walking into the bedroom, she looks around. Nobody has been allowed in the room since his passing. The closet has been emptied after the burning. The only things that remain are the graduation jacket, and a box of hockey cards Denise will inherit when she gets older. Books sit on the shelf that were unboxed after everything was brought back from Toronto. She looks at the computer at the desk after it was blessed by sweet grass. Angie sits on the bed, trying hard not to cry. The familiar quilt his grandmother made for him years before is soft. She's mostly tired from the quick trip to Toronto and back. Walt's mother sits down next to Angie, hugging her, thanking her for going all the way out there to pick up the glasses. She smiles at Angie. "He's here." Angie feels it, too, just like she did the night before—an airy sensation brushing up against her back. It's a cool, faint breeze that reminds her of wind in September or the times she would stand at the bridge and take pictures. Angie takes the glasses out of her pocket, and she tells them how nice James was, how the glasses were found under the bed.

Angie gets up from the bed and puts the glasses on the desk. "Everything is all here now, and you are home, Walt. I miss you so much. We miss you so much. I hope this brings you peace."

Walt's dad puts the lock on the door again, Angie goes to the bathroom to wash her face and hide her tears from the rest of the family. She looks in the mirror, so tired, exhausted, and sad. Forcing a smile, she stops, realizing she looks like a weirdo. The mirror doesn't have towels blocking the reflection anymore. Angie leaves the bathroom and sees the padlock on the door. Before leaving, she gives Denise the hockey jersey she picked up in Vancouver, and Denise happily puts it on like it was draft day. Walt's dad offers Angie a ride down to her house, but she wants to walk instead. The poor kids won't be sliding now that the roads have been sanded, not until the next snowfall or freezing rain comes along. It strikes Angie how life has returned to normal in the tiny village, and how quiet it is compared to Toronto. She notices the sounds of power saws in the distance preparing firewood, kids laughing up at the school, and traffic of people going to or returning from Hazelton. Reality isn't so muted anymore now that everything is done, that he is buried, and can hopefully find peace. Angie turns around, looking at the house. She thinks they'll be all right, that they're strong, and that everyone is there for each other.

Angie gets home, but the house is empty. She puts wood in the fire catching it just before it goes out. The house is heating up, snug and warm, and she can take a nap before catching up with her mom at dinner. Dinner is good, not like the bad airplane food she had to put up with the past day or the fast food she hoped wouldn't give her food poisoning. Dutifully washing the dishes while her mom works in the office, she notices the change through the kitchen window—the sky is actually clear tonight. After hauling the telescope from the bedroom and positioning it on the back patio, she shovels out a clear spot and looks into the lens up to the skies. Walt's dad used to tease him about using it to spy on pretty girls, it would always make his cheeks red. He loved the telescope so much; it was one of his favorite gifts he had ever received. One perk of living in an isolated village is the absence of light pollution, and the place was great for astronomy buffs if the weather was cooperative. Angie stares at the half moon, marveling at the detail and craters, and her mom joins her in the dark looking up at the sky. Not expecting it, the sky begins crying. Once in a while Angie can see the fiery streak of falling stars briefly passing through the lens. She can't track where they fall or if they made it to the ground. They look at the nighttime show with their naked eyes instead. Angie's mom tells her, "Make a wish, sweetie," but realizes what she said and apologizes. Angie only has one wish tonight, and it will never come true.

December

The siren blares loudly throughout the village, waking her from sleep; she sits up frantic, hoping it's not another death in the community. There's always been this superstition that deaths happen in groups, and people were waiting for the next event to happen after Walt was buried in November. There have been no more hauntings reported to Walt's parents since. No sightings of *Lulacs* (ghosts). Life in Gitsegukla has returned to normal as people look forward to Christmas and the New Year. Michelle would later tell Angie the siren was just some stupid kid trying to light the gazebo bus stop on fire who would later get an earful from his parents. Incidentally, it was the same kid Peter beat up the night of the Smoke Feast. Angie doesn't have time to admire the tree she put up with her mom the night before. Whereas she used to lounge around on the couch without purpose, she actually has paying work, a side job to help fund her Christmas plans. Standing up on the couch she reaches to straighten out the star before leaving the house. It's a quick walk up to the Band Office to install security software and update the staff's web browsers, uninstalling any malware or toolbars they have inadvertently caught. Then after that, a quick walk up to the school to upgrade the hard drives on the library computers. After her short work day is over half an hour past three, she walks down with little excited kids who think she's so cool because she fixed the computers and installed games for them to play at lunch or recess.

She stops at Walt's house before she goes home to have dinner with her mom. Stephanie looks at the calendar, noting how many days are left before Christmas. She shows Denise how many sleeps to go before Santa comes to drop off her presents. She doesn't say it, but Stephanie has been secretly hoping Walt had sent them a Christmas parcel like he did the year before. It surprised everyone when the box showed up the second week of December filled with wrapped presents to put underneath the tree. Her brother thought himself clever not having to race around at the last minute in Terrace to get gifts when he could just stroll up and down Yonge Street instead. Stephanie has given up on that hope. Instead, she looks at the bills for the phone and electricity her dad will pay at the bank at the end of the week. "Do you still have it? The sippy cup he got you and Michelle. The one that you brought with you to the New Year's Dance." Stephanie asks. Angie remembers being naughty and spiking her pop. The cup sits on the shelf in her bedroom, and it reminds her she'll probably do the same thing again at New Year's when they all watch fireworks. Stephanie is wearing the gold earrings her brother sent, a simple, studded pair with a diamond in them. Denise still treasures the white puppet rabbit and gets a kick out of it when Angie tickles her with it or chases her around the house. Stephanie had wished a giant box would be hand delivered by the mail lady. Inside would be gifts and hand-written letters, a final goodbye and a sort of bittersweet Christmas miracle. Angie has been wishing the same, but neither say it aloud.

On the way down to her house Angie passes by the overpass. The urge to space out and count cars is not there anymore as she's grown out of that. It can be someone else's spot now. She sees Michelle racing all the way from the bottom of the hill to meet her at the stairs of the church on a snowmobile. "Cops are responding to a domestic dispute in Kispiox, I can race around for the next hour, since nobody's coming to catch me," she says, zooming up the hill. Angie considered hopping on and going joyriding, but she's not properly dressed for backwoods racing up "the Y." Honestly, Angie is still afraid of falling off and getting hurt. The memory of going hunting with her dad, riding on a snowmobile, falling off the back, and scratching her hands on the icy snow still gives her pause. She's never been a big winter outdoors person, and most of her early childhood memories are of rainy Vancouver.

The evening news announces school will finally return to session for the post-secondary students who have now missed out on half a year of studying. Angie looks forward to getting back into the grind in January. There isn't a lot to do in the village without a job or a serious hobby. Keeping up on hockey or watching movies with Michelle on the weekends fills her time. Angie also has done some reading of the text books she bought in preparation for classes. She's stayed in shape chopping wood and shoveling snow while her mom is at work. She still wants to take Denise out sledding or to make a snowman in their yard. Everyone calls this winter *Gweah* (poor) with how light the snow has actually been, and people fear the weather will get harsh in January to make up for things.

The night isn't a complete bust. Instead of being locked

inside again watching overdramatic crime investigations, Stephanie and Michelle drag Angie to bingo. This is the first bingo Walt's parents have hosted since he died. They are raising funds for the youth soccer team that plays in the spring and summer, and the turnout is huge. It is challenging for Angie to keep up with the caller who reads out the numbers. There are too many cards to dab with the ink, and she has to give up one of her extra bingo cards to Michelle for help. With her load lightened Angie can focus on the numbers, and maybe actually win some games. After the halfway mark on the night's schedule she still hasn't won. Michelle teases Angie for her swearing when she gets close, but other people win.

Angie feels guilty about wanting to win bingo, since she doesn't need the money as much as other people who've filled the hall. She's always had a competitive side that brings out the worst in her. While everyone is outside taking a smoke break she looks around the hall, the full tables of people reminding her of the Feast. Everyone returns to their seats to begin the second half of the scheduled games. Angie is listening to Michelle talk about some of the weirdos who show up at the gas station, to say hi to her while she's at work and asking for her number. Did she just win? Angie looks at the number she dabbed—it matches the number the caller said, and she looks at the checkerboard pattern in surprise. Michelle looks, checking the cards over too. The hall slows down for Angie as she gets into a panic, slightly excited as she blurts out, "Bingo." The caller doesn't hear her. Angie grabs the card with her fist, nearly jumps up out of her seat, and stands up saying, "Bingo!" The amateur theatrics caught the caller's eye, and he stops calling. Michelle smacks Angie's arm, half congratulating her for the win, but also teasing her for what she just did. A young guy takes the card away from Angie and verifies she won. When it's confirmed, there's a murmur of cussing as people toss their cards aside getting ready for the next game. The guy returns and counts out the $1000 Angie won. She sits there, dumbfounded at winning and has stopped paying attention to the next game that is already underway. Michelle is now dabbing the numbers Angie is missing.

Michelle says, "Beginner's luck, so you're buying lunch tomorrow. Now you're a fully-fledged bingo addict who'll keep coming back here to chase the feeling you have right now."

Angie doesn't win anymore bingo, but came close on the "Crazy Y" game. Angie is happy the laptop she wanted to pick up for her mom is practically paid for now. She's also been eyeing a gift for Walt's cousin, Eric. Michelle and Denise's presents are already wrapped and underneath the tree, but she's stumped as to what to get Walt's parents or sister. Normally he would give hints at Christmas time, but now there's no one to help.

The next day, an hour before the sun goes down, Michelle and Angie do the rounds handing out Christmas cards from both their houses. Not everyone in the village will get a card. Angie learned the hard way that some people still harbor ill will to her family. They were extremely rude when she idealistically tried to give every house a card several years prior. Now, only good friends of the family or relatives get cards in this village. It's a nice way to spend the day, walking around, meeting people and saying hi, and everyone is appreciative when receiving the cards. It doesn't take long until some of the older ladies impersonate her bingo dance, bouncing up and down yelling, "Bingo." They playfully ask if there's $1000 in the envelope she gave.

Michelle is slightly embarrassed, and responds, "Yep, she's such a bingo newbie."

The two finish at the top of the village and start walking home. The sky is slightly purple and the mountains are white surrounding the village. It inspires Angie to take a picture. On the way down, Michelle tells the story of the gift Walt gave when he was in grade 9 before Karen moved to the village and stole him away. Michelle unzips the thick winter jacket, grabs Angie's hand, and presses it against her flat, skinny stomach to feel the fabric of the purple sweater. "I used to tease him that he bought me a granny sweater. I always thought it was just too fancy compared to the clothes I normally wear." Michelle kept it in the closet all this time and has only now started wearing it to remember Walt. It stayed boxed up in the closet neatly preserved. Michelle zips up her jacket again. "You need to stop by my house before you head home. She wants to give you something."

The two enter Michelle's house, and see her grandmother is in the kitchen making curry moose stew. Walt's grandmother made the same and invited Angie for dinner a week earlier. It was the best plate she had all month. Angie almost wants to ask to stay, but she has to go with her mom and visit extended family in Hazelton for the evening. Michelle hangs up her jacket and takes off her boots. Angie stands at the doorway not sure if she should follow. Michelle's grandmother joins her at the top of the stairs and stares at Michelle. "Take off my sweater. You should know better than to steal your *Jiitses'* clothes." Her *Jiits* laughs, fully aware it was a gift, and it's one of the rare times Angie sees Michelle blushing from being teased. Michelle's grandmother hands Angie a clear bag of smoked salmon strips made the summer before, *Hooxsw*. The *Hooxsw* strips are big, with no bones, and are a nice, warm, reddish-orange color. Angie can smell the smoky taste before she even puts a small piece in her mouth where it melts—outsiders would call it pseudo salmon jerky. "Make sure you eat it with some Oolichan grease, it'll be even better. Now that will be $100, please." says Michelle's grandmother. She laughs at her joke as she goes back to the kitchen to finish her cooking. It's not hard at all to see where Michelle got her playful spirit or wit, and her big, generous heart. The bag of *Hooxsw* is worth ten times more than what she was teasing at. Angie is still learning how to properly make canned fish in her family's smoke house. Maybe next year they'll teach her how to make her own smoked salmon strips too. Michelle already knows how, since she was taught by her grandparents at a young age, and even knows how to make sweet, golden-brown, fried bread. It takes Angie a while before she recalls how many jars of Oolichan grease are still in their fridge. Once in a while her mom trades fish with her cousin who lives up the Nass. The Nisga'a have perfected the art of extracting grease from Candlefish, which is used to complement some of the foods Gitksan people eat. Oolichan grease is most commonly called *Dillix,* which is great for *Hooxsw* or on top of *Hashbadinner*, and is sometimes used to ease sore throats. Angie realizes she's starving with all the thoughts of food in her head right now. She thanks both of them before leaving—she has to warm up her mom's car for their trip to town.

Angie can't wait to get back home after the visit with cousins in Hagwilget, a decent-sized reserve within Hazelton, so she can check emails from Walt's circle of friends. At the suggestion of James and Talia, they have been sending any pictures they took of him when he was in Toronto. She looks at each one, saving them to a memory card so she can print them the next time they go to Terrace. Angie has been playing email tag with Walt's computer science classmate and friend, Sam, and the two both decide to try video chatting. That worries Angie, because she doesn't know if her internet connection in the village can even manage. It's an upgrade from dial up which they still used until that summer, but it's not as fast as city internet connections. Angie turns on the video chat application and dials Sam. It's only then that Angie remembers the time difference between British Columbia and eastern Canada: they are three hours apart, and on the other side it is midnight. The screen reads, "Connecting to Sam Ryncone," as it makes little, faux, phone call ringing noises. Angie sits there looking at a big black cat staring at her through the screen. "Sam? Nice to meet you. Would you like some milk?"

A voice on the other side answers, "Shoo, bad kitty, go."

The cat jumps off the desk, and Angie can only hear sounds of the door closing in the background and the cat meowing in protest. Angie looks through the digital window into Sam's room. The walls are painted a summer yellow, and on the wall hangs a large Montreal hockey team flag. Angie turns around, looking back at her wall and wondering what Sam could see? Just a blank wall with one lone graduation photo taken at K'San Museum on a hot June day.

Sam giggles when Angie turns around from comparing the rooms. Angie wasn't sure what to expect when she saw Sam, and it turns out Sam is a girl her age. Her hair is cut short, light red, and the tips lift up at her ears. Angie can see freckles behind the glasses she is wearing, as well as her dark blue eyes. She is wearing white pajamas with printed rabbit designs—the kind they draw in children's books. The two introduce themselves and then sit quietly lit by the glow of their respective laptop screens. Angie had always assumed Sam was a guy. Walt would mention going out to movies or the bar with James, Jared, and Sam on weekends. "How is everyone back there? Everyone misses him here; it's so hard walking back from class and not being able to visit him at his dorm anymore. When news got around about what happened that morning it absolutely broke my heart. I ended up taking three weeks off, but had to come back for end-of-term exams. I wish I had gotten to meet you when you showed up for his glasses." Angie explains that everyone is still hurting, but everyone is adapting. It gets harder for everyone with Christmas coming up. Multitasking, Sam is clicking with her mouse on the other end, and the notifications pop up on Angie's screen. "Those are all the photos I have of him when he was here. You can share those with his parents and keep them for yourself, too, if you want. It's not much, since he wasn't big on having his picture taken. I'd just goof around and take them when he wasn't looking." Sam explains she wanted to come visit to pay her respects a week after the funeral. "I couldn't find it on the map. Gitsegukla. I hope I'm saying that right. I couldn't find it." Angie replies that no, it's not on the map officially, but if she searches for Skeena Crossing it will turn up the location of Gitsegukla easily. Skeena Crossing being the marker of where the train bridge crosses the Skeena River.

Angie's imagination runs away from her as she stares at Sam through the screen. Maybe Walt was dating her, and they were serious and even planning on marriage. Maybe she would come out to the village to visit for Christmas, and by New Year's would break the happy news she was actually pregnant with Walt's baby. Even though he wasn't in this world anymore, he might have left something beautiful for everyone, and the loss wouldn't feel so final. Sam interrupts to tell her she needs to go get some water and will be right back.

"Do you want to know how we met?" Sam asks as she takes a sip of water. Angie is genuinely curious, since Walt was always shy with girls. Sam and Walt had computer science class together, and English literature. "I like to think I caught his eye during the first week of school, in computer science class. My friend Janine pointed him out, said he was checking me out from the back corner of the auditorium while we sat near the front. I think Janine laughing set things backwards for him." Sam later learned, months later, that when Janine giggled that morning he put up his defenses. Sam continues, "I tried so many times to get his attention after that first week.

I would cross the length of the row he sat in and he'd be so friendly in letting me by, but would never make eye contact— even when I leaned in too close nearly bumping my chest into his face. We both lived in the same dorm building and would walk the same path after class. I even tried slowing down my pace to let him catch up to me, since I was always a fast walker racing to get to classes on time. This one time in October we were walking side by side just so briefly. But before I could say hi he veered off into some random building to give me space." Sam stops and smiles, then starts speaking again, "I hope he didn't feel like I was tormenting him as I tried to get closer. In November, I had a two-part plan. During computer science with each lecture I would move up a couple of rows until we were in the same one. And then I would inch several seats over, a little at a time. On the day I was going to sit next to him classes were cancelled because of a storm. So as a last-ditch chance in English class I plainly wrote my number on a flier and gave it to him, and he thought he was supposed to pass it along and did."

Angie laughs, and blurts out, "*Gooch*, oh my god he was so *Gooch*."

Sam asks what that word means. Angie tells her it means 'clumsy' or 'inept'. Sam practices saying the new word she heard. She starts, "School was ending and I went out with friends dancing. At the end of the night I decided to stop for pizza. I wasn't exactly black-out drunk or slurring, but I was high and enjoying pizza at my table. These two frat creeps approached me, trying their lines and wanting to get me to come back with them to some party they were having at their house. Nope, I know better than to listen to those probable rapists. They wouldn't leave me alone even after politely telling them I had other plans, and that I was waiting for friends. I wanted to eat my pizza and get home safely." Sam talks about stopping with eye contact and staring at her pizza, extending her leg so they couldn't sit in the booth seats opposite of her. Sam said she considered calling up Janine to pick her up or even making a run for it. "Just as I was about to dial I saw him enter and stand at the line waiting to make his order. In that moment, I was able to make eyes to him and silently ask for help, and he came to my rescue. Walt came over and said hi to the two guys, and loudly apologized for being late, but he, along with James and Talia, they were finally there. He waved to James and Talia for effect." The two creeps left Sam alone, and Walt took that as his cue to leave too. "Please stay," Sam says, the memory still fresh in her mind, "and he did. James and Talia ordered him a pizza, then walked off and left leaving us alone." The two quietly ate their pizza before speaking. "I asked him for his name, and he tells me it's Bob. I remember laughing, saying that's my cat's name too. That had to be a sign, right? Bob, bob cat, I did these weird cosmic association everything's all connected things in my head. Then he told me his real name." Sam explained to Walt all the things she had tried doing to get his attention over those last few months and was embarrassed he missed out on the obvious clues. The two finished their pizza and strolled back to the dorm building, Angie pictures them standing outside the front entrance with a light snow falling down on them. "He walked me home, holding my arm so I wouldn't slip or fall. I put my number into his phone and punched his arm, making him promise to call, which he did innocently the next afternoon. That was how we first met, and when I knew I had met a truly special person who I now find myself missing so hard."

Sam starts tearing up and leaves to hide her crying. Angie knows that feeling all too well. When Sam returns composed and with a face washed, she says, "We never dated. I wanted to, but I'd only learn in January he had just split up with a girl named Karen. He was fun to be around—he had a weird sense of humor and would be the only person who'd get my jokes or references. I accepted that, but hoped one day we would see if we could get beyond being friends. So, we'd occasionally study for classes, or James and Talia would invite me along for outings and try to pair us together officially. The timing wasn't right, but it is what it is." Angie's fantastical runaway happy ending is dashed. Sam can see the disappointment in her face, she says, "I wish things were different too. I really do. I wish he was still here, and that I could pop in his doorway and we'd play video games in the common room." Angie finds herself thinking the same, of popping up at the house and the two of them playing pool in the basement like they used to. "I need to go to sleep. We should try to chat again, at a normal hour. Maybe you can tell me more about your time with him on your side of the world. Good night, Angie."

* * *

Days later, the shopping rush at the mall catches Angie by surprise. Angie never expected the hallways to be full, since most people do their shopping at the two big department stores at the edges of Terrace. Once in a while Angie sees the faces of former opponents she played at the all-native basketball tournament hosted in Prince Rupert every spring. They don't recognize her, and it strikes her that some of them are now with children. Stephanie leaves Angie to herself and darts off into the crowd to do her shopping, putting emphasis on her not following Stephanie and cheating. Angie has her tiny list to pick up, and thankfully the laptop is still in stock. Angie sees Eric's gift on the shelf too, a fun action game that has received a lot of good reviews, and picks him up a game for the console he inherited from Walt. After paying high school kids to wrap her presents she sits down at the bench, playing her lottery numbers that are drawn every four minutes. She only makes out with $4 in winnings. On her way to the food court she passes a novelty shop and spots two pairs of cat ear headbands—they're perfect stocking stuffers for Michelle and Denise. Stephanie catches up with Angie, asking if they're ready to hit the last store before grabbing dinner.

As soon as they get to the front door of the box mart Stephanie is already gone again. Angie picks up a hand basket to do some light shopping for personal items, plus picking up stuff her mom asked for before they left the village. Angie finds her favorite soaps and shampoos, slowly taking her time rather than being stuck waiting at the entrance of the store for Stephanie, who has the car keys. In that brief alone time, she intentionally wanders to the pharmacy section and tries to figure out which brand of laxatives her mother wanted. It's then she hears a box fall over in the next aisle, the hollow sound of vitamins or headache pills bouncing against the plastic like a baby rattle. Angie hears Karen's voice cuss briefly. It excites Angie, and she races to see her friend again, she says, "Karen? I didn't know you were back already." Angie hugs her, and continues, "Holy cow, it's so good to see you again."

Karen hugs Angie hard before letting her go, she replies, "I got back yesterday. I was only in the village for a few hours before my aunt came to pick me up. I'll be staying here in Terrace for the holidays."

Angie knows why—everyone knows why. Karen's parents have gone into one of their extended drinking benders that is usually followed by public fighting and an anonymous call to the police to keep the peace. It's just then that Angie realizes she's still holding the laxatives in hand and tries to discreetly drop them in the hand basket without drawing attention to her purchase. The two catch up on what's happened in the past month. The hauntings, her sudden trip to Toronto, winning bingo, and meeting Sam via video chat.

"Sam is a nice girl. I was jealous when he mentioned her and introduced us on a video chat in September. I don't know about her little boy haircut, but she seemed friendly," Karen says as she plays soccer with the box of pills that fell to the floor.

Angie senses irritation and upset with Karen—maybe bringing up Sam is a sore subject right now. Angie asks, "Do you want to meet us for dinner? At the Chinese place by the hospital. We're stopping there before heading home." Karen says she'll think about it, check with her aunt to see if she made plans, and will call to confirm or not. As Karen hugs Angie goodbye once more, it's only then Angie notices her friend's eyes are on the verge of welling up with tears. It makes Angie sad seeing her friend at a low point, Karen dealing with the drama thanks to her drunken parents, losing the love of her life, and not getting to spend Christmas with her friends. That feeling of isolation and loneliness that piles on reminds Angie of the time she stood out there on the overpass before Walt came along and saved her. The thought crosses into Angie's mind instantly, and she runs clumsily into the main aisles after Karen, nearly tripping over a mother and her kid. Angie catches up to Karen as she waits in line to pay for her things. "I don't know what's going on with you right now, Karen, whether you're hurting like us back at home. Walt told me how cool it was of your aunt to take you in when things were rough at home, but you always felt like you were intruding on her life. When I needed a place to be, Walt and his family always took me in, no matter what. It was great having a place to go to and feel like I belonged. We've never been that close, I know that, but if you want you can come back—there's an open guest room at my house. All of us would love to have you back in the village this Christmas. So if that's something you'd be interested in, all you have to do is say yes."

Angie looks into the guest room, curious, the thick comforter is inviting, the dresser is waiting to be filled with clothes, and she stands smiling after preparing the room. Karen agreed to come back to the village for a few days before Christmas in time for the planned friends and family dinner being hosted in the basement of Walt's house. Karen would have loved to come home with Stephanie and Angie on the spot, but promised her cousins a long overdue visit when she wrapped up school; she promised to take them to the movies and bowling. Angie takes a moment to put the presents underneath the tree. She carefully places pre-wrapped gifts for her mom, Walt's parents, Stephanie, and Karen next to the other gifts. Once Karen accepted her offer she quickly searched for a thick Turkish bathrobe Angie hoped Karen would like and then had it wrapped. Angie talks with her mom about how terrible the roads were and how Stephanie drove carefully when they hit patches of icy road. They cussed the highway department for not salting or sanding the roads enough. Angie's mom is curious about her soon-to-be guest, as she never really knew Karen other than that she dated Walt for a few years. Angie quietly explains, "I felt something inside me when we met to-night. Something felt wrong about leaving her in Terrace this holiday. I'm sorry I didn't ask you in advance, and I hope you don't mind. Karen is a great girl—you'll like her when she gets back to the village next week. It'll only be for a few days before we all have to go back to school."

Angie retreats to her room, sitting on her bed and look-ing at the newly developed pictures Sam and James sent from Toronto. Once in a while she busts out laughing at the pic-tures. Walt making weird faces when being forced to eat a bizarre looking Tuna casserole. Walt finding a sign in one of Toronto's parks that graphically says, "No skateboarding dogs listening to music while getting drunk." Or seeing the picture of Walt doing a faux native blockade in the middle of Bloor

Street, similar to the blockades the Gitksan people would do to protest excess logging or mining projects on traditional lands. All of these photos have their place in the album Angie has created in her cousin's memory. Angie stares at the last photo taken of Walt before his passing, snapped by Sam a few days before Halloween. In it, he sits looking out the window; the sun made the light clouds pink in the distance, and there are sharp shadows cast by neighboring buildings. Walt hadn't known that would be the last photo taken of him, if he did, he probably would have gone for something goofy or even somber. It's just a simple photo of him leaning against the couch in the common room peering out at mountains that don't exist. "He always stared out west. Back to where he came from. He missed you, his sister, his little niece, and parents. The adjustment to life in Toronto still bothered him, and he never forgot where he came from. That's what I always thought when I looked at this photo. I do the same after classes, I look east, out my window, wondering how my parents are doing in Montreal." Those were the words Sam sent when she attached the photo in the email to Angie. She places that photo on the last page of the album and then turns the page to the beginning where his life started. A worn, faded, slightly bent photo Stephanie had given when she learned of Angie's project. Angie was gifted a photo of Walt hours after being born at the Hazelton hospital. His grandfather had gone to the nearest convenience store just to buy a camera to capture his first grandson. He looked so tiny with his black hair and wrapped in a cotton blanket with blue stripes. The album now has a beginning and an end, and she wonders how long it will take to fill it up.

Before going to bed Angie realizes it feels like it's been a while since she's seen her best friend. With holidays, shopping, and work they've been out of sync. After getting dressed she walks across the street, hoping she isn't waking them up—the lights look dim in the living room. Michelle's grandmother opens the door and lets Angie in. As Angie walks downstairs, and Michelle's grandmother upstairs to her room to sleep, she can hear music from the stereo. Angie sees her ruined face when Michelle opens the bedroom door and the smell of alcohol follows. Angie's instincts kick in and she grabs Michelle and holds her, the soft sniffling becoming loud sobbing. The two make their way to the couch in the corner, and Angie turns down the music for the sake of her grandmother who's probably trying to sleep upstairs. The sadness sunk in at the end of Michelle's work shift. She was fine up until she flipped the channel and a movie came on. It reminded her of the time Walt and Michelle spent watching late night movies together, when Walt comforted Michelle after she lost her grandfather. So Michelle came home, fired up the sad ballad music, and opened up the bottle of vodka Doug gave her for her birthday. She didn't mean to get so down and promises to apologize to her grandmother in the morning. Michelle laughs, she says, "He's going to get so fat wherever he is out there. All this week we've been making food for him and putting it in the fire. Tonight, my grandmother made her special golden mushroom and sausage plate. The night before, salmon steak cooked over flames with roasted potatoes. You were there when she was making moose curry stew." Michelle offers Angie a drink, but she's okay and refuses. It's not that Walt's death means the end of Angie drinking or having fun, but she doesn't know how emotional she would get if she did drink. Sometimes she still struggles to keep composure when she finds herself missing him. Even when she sees little things, where her first instinct is to call Walt at his house to change the television channel to watch a dumb commercial, or email him a link to some cat video. Michelle starts singing a parody song Walt wrote when he was still in high school. "I pee in the stream, that is what we do, no one sees us now, maybe go number two, don't have teepee, in these dark woods, is that a bear over there, oh crap, it's probably time to leave now uh-huh." The two break out into fits of laughter, and even more laughing when they remember him dragging Michelle up to sing the duet at the karaoke bar in Terrace confusing everyone at first, but winning over the drunken crowd. "So *maluu*, I never knew someone that crazy," Michelle says as she gets up to turn off the stereo. Michelle assures Angie she'll be okay. Angie goes upstairs to get Michelle a cup of water and leaves it at the nightstand. "It's okay to feel sad, Angie, you don't have to be so strong. If you're hurting then you're hurting, and maybe you can let the hurt heal." The two say good night, and Angie goes back to her room across the street, looking out the window to make sure Michelle's light stays off, and occasionally peering down the road to the graveyard.

* * *

Denise's little bare feet make padding noises on the kitchen tiles as she chases Angie around the house with the rabbit puppet in hand. She couldn't be any happier having the house so full and everyone playing with her. Every once in a while, she needs to be pried away from the Christmas tree because she's shaking boxes, clearly excited to open the presents with her name on them. Stephanie and her father are working on a project that should be ready by the time Christmas rolls around. Walt's mom checks in on Angie to see how she's doing, if she's happy to finally be going back to school after the New Year. She's also curious about the red-headed girl people have been mentioning, so Angie explains who Sam was to Walt in Toronto and that they were good friends. She can tell his mother hoped there was more to that story too.

Nadine says, "The little birdy across the street told us about your album. We want you to have this."

Walt's mother goes to the kitchen table and grabs an envelope to hand to Angie. She sits next to Angie, waiting for her to open it up. Inside is a thick bundle of photos selected by Walt's parents, of their son in various states of growing up. Nadine tries to explain what was going on when each photo was taken. Angie is familiar with the newer set of pictures. Graduation post party pictures in Walt's back yard, snapshots of everyone at the hospital waiting for Denise to be born, and Walt holding his niece for the first time. There are many pictures of Walt with his grandparents. Walt in the front yard of the house, riding bikes with Doug and Peter, after school. A few hunting shots of Walt standing alongside his grandfather and uncle up the mountain, each holding a kill. Angie smiles seeing Walt trying so hard to hold up a groundhog he shot, and in the fuzzy distance she can see Gitsegukla in the background behind the hunters. Angie hugs Nadine, thanking her for being so generous, and at first insists they shouldn't be giving away original copies, offering to make digital copies and then returning them. Walt's mother isn't concerned about such things, since they still have the negatives to most of their photos safely stored away in the closet. Stephanie has been scanning the pictures and storing them digitally, too, just in case.

Denise goes to bed on her own proudly saying, "Santa, two sleeps."

Angie is shown the picture of Denise sitting on Santa's lap at the village Christmas concert up at the school. Angie's mom always teases her about how violently she cried when they tried taking her picture with some weird fat guy dressed in red when she was little.

Walking home, it strikes Angie how powdery fresh the latest snowfall is, and it hasn't been plowed or sanded by the highway department yet. The sky is clear, and the partial moon illuminates the landscape. Angie wonders if this is what being on the moon is like; she looks back at the fresh imprints her boots have been making. The driveway will need to be shoveled in the morning unless her mom hires someone. Michelle's house lights are off—they've gone to sleep early. The whole village is quiet with no cars driving or snowmobiles racing around. No dogs barking. No sound of people listening to music loudly down the street. There isn't even the sound of kids playing street hockey on this Saturday night, emulating the broadcasted games they watched on television. Peaceful silence, except for the muffled crunch of Angie falling back in her front yard. Angie is thankful she didn't fatally impale herself with any sharp objects buried under the snow like a rake or sprinklers. This would be her indie movie moment they'd show in the trailers. Just her and the goddamned snow, now sneaking under her jacket collar, staring at the stars above. It doesn't feel so bad after a while. The cold and the light breeze are tolerable. Up above is the constellation of Orion, over there the Big Dipper, and a few passing satellites sail above the sky. Walt made her do this one time, and the memory comes back to her in the backyard of Walt's house. Stephanie spent one winter making a homemade backyard rink with her dad. It had snowed over the surface, and instead of shoveling it Walt plopped down and recited all the astronomy facts he learned when he got the telescope. Angie remembers thinking it was childish then to lay there in the snow, goofing around making snow angels. She thinks, "What the hell," and makes a new one before getting up and brushing the snow off her jacket. Angie looks down at the lone snow angel; she made it for him. Angie enters her house and takes off her soaking jacket and boots, hanging them up to dry. One month has passed, and Angie wonders if this will get easier, but she really doesn't know.

Christmas is now one day away, not that they're counting sleep anymore. Many people in the village listen for the siren to go off, sometimes followed by early fireworks, and open their presents at midnight. Angie lays in bed fighting the onset of a cold that's trying to form. Her mom just fed her a hot plate of seafood and salmon soup, an orange, and a spoon with melted Oolichan grease in place of medicine. "Silly girl, making snow angels when it's -20 out," she kindly scolds her daughter before going to visit relatives. After drifting out of a nap she wants so badly to open the window, since the heat from the wood stove is unbearable, but she was ordered not to. She can hear the clanking of steel as someone comes in the basement of the house and fills up the stove and then goes out the back door. It's then that she hears the shoveling outside, the scraping of frozen snow being brushed to the sides in a neat little mound. She stands up on her bed, looking out. It's Doug. Angie gets dressed and goes to the front door, she looks at her college buddy, a guy she dated briefly, but they were never a match.

Angie asks, "Doug, what are you doing?"

Doug explains he put out an advertisement at the band office billboard, leaving his number to do on-call shoveling or wood chopping. He was keeping busy and making a little money for when they get back to school. Angie's mom hired him when she saw him finishing up across the street at Michelle's place. She invites him in after he's done to warm up with some coffee or tea, and she asks him not to shovel anything on top of her goofy yard art, on Walt's snow angel. After Doug is done he knocks on the door and lets himself inside after pounding his boots at the frame, so as to not track any snow inside, before he takes them off at the entrance. Angie has finished washing her plate and cup, feeling better already. "Sick, eh?" Doug asks as he sits at the table. The two have talked little since the passing of their friend. Doug still looks out his bedroom window, hoping to see Walt in the back shoveling snow, playing with Denise, or hauling in firewood for his dad. There's that absence that's too hard to ignore for him. He leaves that unsaid and instead thanks Angie for paying him and giving him a cup of lightly sugared tea from the pot. Doug refuses soup and bread because he needs to hit the next house on his schedule. As he leaves, it strikes Angie that he wanted to say more but didn't, and that maybe he'll open up more when they're back in school. The two live in the same wing of the Prince George dorm and bump into each other often. Still under the weather, Angie crawls back into bed for another nap.

Disappointed, Angie receives the news that Karen will be staying in Terrace on Christmas Eve, but will try very hard to show up for the dinner tomorrow. Michelle calls up from across the street, asking what Angie's plans are for the evening. Michelle explains that her grandmother always opens presents on Christmas morning, she says, "It's what good people do—no cheating and opening everything at midnight and then being disappointed on Christmas Day with nothing to do." Angie slowly agrees with that assessment, but there's no changing things now. Michelle's grandmother will be in bed by 10pm after watching some Christmas movies or variety specials.

Angie invites Michelle to join her at Walt's house, she says, "You can cheat and open some presents early. Come on, it'll be fun."

Michelle happily agrees, and visibly waves goodbye through the living room window as they hang up.

Angie, tired, is yawning as they sit on the couch counting down the clock to midnight. Everyone is digesting and under the effects of the large turkey dinner Walt's mother cooked for Christmas Eve, and Stephanie asks her mom what will they do for tomorrow's gathering. "Leftovers, macaroni and cheese, bologna sandwiches, and microwave pizza," she jokes in response. Stephanie, needing the bathroom, gently lifts the sleeping Denise off her lap and rests her on the couch. Michelle is out on the porch, sharing a smoke with Walt's dad. Angie eyes the tree, ensuring Michelle won't be left out when the time comes, that there will be gifts for her to open along with everyone else. When Michelle comes in following Walt's dad, Angie just notices she's an inch taller. Has she been growing or is he now shrinking in size as old age comes along? Walt's father doesn't seem so old, since he's only in his mid-fifties. Michelle sits down next to Walt's mom.

Nadine says, "I went with him that day we got your sweater. I was thinking let's get something young and cool that you'd like. He had his heart set on fancy and grand, and the price didn't matter, since he wanted to get you something special."

Michelle looks down at her Christmas shirt, proud. She took a few years to appreciate it, but eventually she grew to love it. Angie checks down to her side and sees the tiny eyes looking up, blank at first, but now gazing at the clock. Denise closes her eyes, trying to extend her nap. Walt's dad takes that cue and goes downstairs. He exits the house, and Angie can see him walking down the street to the fire hall. People in the village aren't allowed to ring the siren whenever they want, it's only for emergencies or announcing deaths. At Christmas, someone eventually finds their way to the hall to signal the siren. When the blaring stops, families across the village begin the hour-long fun of handing presents to each other, opening them, and parents trying to get their kids to sleep at a respectable hour.

The siren rings, and even though she was expecting it, it still made Angie jump. She could feel little Denise jump up excited and clapping her hands, yelling, "Santa, Santa, Santa!" There's a loud pounding on the door.

Walt's mom in a playful-sounding voice asks Denise, "Who's that? Someone's at the door Denise!"

The two run to the top of the staircase and look down. Denise screams when she sees a man wearing a red coat, with a red hat, and a big fluffy white beard.

Santa takes a moment to take off his boots, and laughs as he walks up the stairs, Santa says, "Ho ho ho, Merry Christmas. Who's that I see, is that Denise? Has Denise been a good girl this year?"

Carrying a velvet red bag on his shoulder, filled with gifts, Santa leads everyone to the living room. Denise jumps on his lap excitedly, impatient and wanting everyone to take the picture already. She kisses Santa on the cheek when he hands her a present. She runs back to her mom with a giant box with red and green wrapping. It doesn't take the little girl long to open it and find a giant doll house and collection of dolls. Denise and Stephanie retreat to the dining room area to unpack everything and assemble the toy. Next, Michelle sits on Santa's lap, Santa declares, "Oh, you've gotten very big this year. Have you been a good girl?" Angie takes a quick photo of the two before he hands Michelle a gift.

Michelle sits next to Angie and opens it up, then she screams, "Dolly, dolly, dolly," and runs to Denise to play with her on the other side of the room.

"Come on, little girlie, don't be shy." Angie sits on Santa's lap, and she can hear him strain, causing her to laugh and apologize. The two pause as they have their picture taken. "You've been a good girl this year, right? I don't need to check my list. You're not smoking anymore. Have you been good to your mom?"

Angie replies, "Yes, Santa, I try to be." Reaching into the bag he pulls out a small box the size of a finger. It is wrapped in gold, with a fine red bow.

"Santa and Mrs. Santa both thought you were a good girl this year. They want you to be safe out there when you go to school, and this is a special present just for you."

Angie looks at the box, concerned, asking what she was given. Santa hugs her and bellows out it's time to go back to his reindeer. He takes a bite out of the cookie and thanks Denise for handing him milk. He stomps downstairs and out the yard, Denise watching through the patio window and waving bye. Stephanie closes the curtain, and they refocus on assembling the giant house.

Michelle joins Angie at the couch, she asks, "What did Santa give you?"

Angie answers, "I don't know," as she slowly pulls the ribbon off the box. Angie can feel all the eyes in the room watching. Opening the box and pulling aside the white tissue paper, she finds two things, a folded piece of paper, and under it two pairs of keys. The key-chain on one side shows the house clan emblem of the Grouse. Angie flips it over and sees his face smiling up at her. It takes a while to register, and a tear runs down her cheek before she realizes the gift that was given. Hugging Walt's mom Angie breaks down into tears—she can't accept the gift, it doesn't feel right. Angie goes downstairs as she hears Walt's father sneak in the back-door after changing out of the Santa outfit. "I can't. I can't take this gift, it's too much." The two grieving parents hug her, keeping her standing up, and assure her it's what they want. They lead her to the garage, looking at the black SUV once given to Walt on his graduation day. It has been kept tucked safely in the garage during the winter and hadn't been touched since he died.

Gilbert says, "The pink slip and the keys are yours. I had it tuned up this week by Jerry when you and Stephanie were shopping in Terrace. It runs perfectly, and there's a fresh set of winter tires already on it."

Walt's mom reasons with her, Nadine says, "Him taking you in that night was not an accident. It was meant to happen, the two cousins finding each other, being there for each other. In you, we found another amazing kid to take in as our own, someone who's growing up to be an amazing young woman. Just like Stephanie and Denise upstairs, you'll always be one of our baby girls. We want to do this, Angie."

Walt's father continues, "Your car is a piece of crap. It won't do for the trips you take between here and Prince

George, especially in January and February. None of us want to worry about you, which is why we're giving you this. We knew this big beast would protect Walt out on the road when he drove it, so we want you to be safe out there too. Please, take it. Just one thing that we ask of you, don't drink and drive, and no texting while driving, either."

Angie thanks them and hopes they can feel her gratitude with how hard and long she hugs them, and they walk up the stairs regaining composure so as not to worry Denise. "Oh man, did I miss Santa?"

Denise runs to the tree and grabs a present for her grand-father, saying, "Present, your present!"

It's so hard for her when she puts the truck into reverse, and they watch her back out as she opens and closes the ga-rage door. Michelle, next to her, waves bye to Denise who got cranky and wanted sleep. "I was there the afternoon they smoked it. It has been blessed and will take you safely to where you need to go Angie. He'll be watching over you," Michelle says as she buckles her seatbelt. "Oh man, I've always wanted this sweet dolly," she says, laughing as she waves it in Angie's face. The two pull into the driveway of Angie's house and stand outside. In the distance, some kids can be heard sledding with their new sleds, and a couple of houses down music blares as a family celebrates Christmas more than most. This is still a bittersweet surprise for Angie. Michelle breaks the tension by making her kiss the doll good night before she goes home to sleep. She looks forward to celebrating Christ-mas with her grandmother bright and early. Angie's mom is snoring loudly down the hall when she enters her house, undisturbed by the siren. She fills up the stove with the wood Doug cut earlier. At first, she sits on the bed crying, trying to hide it in the pillow. Then the memories of fun they all had in the truck come back to her in bits and pieces. The trips they would take out to Prince Rupert to see movies that hadn't made it to the Terrace movie theater yet. The drive up to Alaska when they all went berry picking. And the casual drives to Hazelton to pick up junk food and rent movies with Michelle and Peter in the backseat. Angie didn't realize it at the time, but when Michelle waved the doll in her face she remembered his scent just briefly, a whiff of the cologne Karen gave him on his birthday. She finds some calm as she lies on her bed the opposite way, looking out at the sky, which is partly cloudy, and thinking about where her cousin is. Angie wishes him a Merry Christmas hoping he is happy wherever he is out there.

The shaking bed method has always annoyed Angie in the morning. Instead of saying her name or touching her arm, Angie's mom has secretly enjoyed rattling her daughter's bed when she sleeps in. Even though it is Christmas and a holiday, cooking needs to be done. Stephanie is coordinating the menu and has hinted it would be okay for them to make a giant pot of homemade chow mein. The two exchange presents and thank each other for the gifts. Angie volunteers to finish cooking the meal so her mom can get acquainted with the new laptop and transfer her files to the new one. In the middle of stirring the boiling noodles and browning the hamburger chunks the doorbell rings. Angie opens it, and notices the roads are plowed and sanded; she smiles and greets Karen, who has finally returned to the village. "I thought I'd drop by. I hope you had a good Christmas last night with everyone," Karen says as she's invited in. The two sit on the couch, staring at the tree. "I'm sorry I flaked out and didn't make it home. It's kind of hard finding a ride out here and I'm not dumb enough to hitchhike. I won't be joining you as a guest, my parents wanted me back home so my aunt drove me back. It was all right, doing a Christmas breakfast with pancakes. Opening presents. It's so hard being there, though, wondering when the other shoe will drop and they go back to the beer I know is hidden in their closet." Angie reiterates that the door is always open if she needs a place to retreat to. "You have such a big heart, you and your mom. I thank you for the offer. I got you guys this." Karen opens up the plastic bag she was carrying and takes out a wrapped gift that looks like a television show collection on DVD. Angie remembers, rushes to the tree, and gives Karen her present. The long, thick robe is a hit, Karen loves the gift, and she thanks Angie. The two move to the kitchen as Angie tends to the cooking, Karen pitches in, washing and chopping the mushrooms. "It was hard walking up to your house just now, I have to be honest. Seeing his truck parked almost made me forget he was gone. I was about to run to the door to see you two, and then I remembered." After the ingredients are prepared they put them into the wok to stir fry them together.

Once in a while Angie stirs it and pours a tiny amount of soy sauce for color, she says, "Everyone keeps calling it Soya sauce." The two move back to the couches as the food is nearly ready.

"Have you ever seen a haunting with your own eyes, Angie?" Karen asks seriously. Angie only recounts hearing things fall over or seeing weird things out of the corner of her eyes. "I don't know how to say this without you calling the cops and having me locked up, but I saw one." Angie asks what she means. Karen answers, "The fight I had with my parents was so harsh, things were said that shouldn't have been. I got picked up by my aunt after hitchhiking to Kitwanga gas station. I didn't want to be here at all. Everything compounding on top of each other: school debts, my math grades, all the drama with my parents, and this unbearable regret about how I ended things with Walt. Worse, what I said to him to make it a clean break." Angie consoles her; they still managed to be friends through it all. "Just so briefly, a plan ran through my head. I'd book a room at a motel on the edge of Terrace, tell my aunt I wanted some alone time, and I'd just go to sleep. Not wake up. Like he did." The calm smile on Angie's face disappears as the words register in her head, and her eyes widen and eyebrows contort. "And so there I was. At the store in the pharmacy aisle. It was supposed to be a neat in and out without anybody noticing. Just like that, just as I was extending my hand to the box of sleeping pills I planned on taking, it happened. Plop, the sound of the cardboard hitting the linoleum tiles and the pills rattling around inside. I stared at them on the floor, confused. What the hell happened? And soon after, you come around the corner holding your laxatives, and that brief window I had closed." Angie asks if Karen's okay, and her first instinct is to ask her if she wants to talk, but they're already doing that. "I will not lie to you, Angie. I was going to do it. The box popping off the shelf changed things. It wasn't until I got home to my aunt's place and sat in the bathroom pretending to shower that I thought about it on the toilet seat. It was him, wasn't it? I want to believe it was him that night telling me: *No. No, it will not be like this, you will live.* And you coming along being so sweet wasn't an accident, either. Your kind words and invitation. It was an intervention I needed so badly." Angie sits, speechless, not sure how to reply. "I told my aunt all this the next day. We booked an appointment, and I've been prescribed some anti-depressants after the doctor made me take a test. My aunt is making me see a therapist when I get back to school. Your face looks so worried right now, please don't be. I feel like my life has been touched, like a toy train that has been put back on the tracks." Angie offers to be there whenever Karen wants to talk, at any time day or night. "Both of you saved me that night. That's why I came down here to visit. Thank you so much, Angie, I needed you to know that." Karen hugs Angie before she leaves. Angie wants to tie her down and keep her locked away for her own good. She does not know how to deal with the very real threat of suicide. It leaves her sick inside. She has the realization she did that to her parents at the Memorial. While the chow mein keeps warm on the stove she goes to her mom to apologize.

The basement recreation room surprises Angie when she enters. Stephanie and her mom spent the morning decorating and arranging the tables and chairs for the small friends and family Christmas dinner, a mini feast that has been planned a month in advance. The pool table has been covered with a white tablecloth, and already there's cooked food wrapped up and waiting to be served. Stephanie shows Angie how everyone will walk around the table counter clockwise, grabbing what foods they want and returning to the main tables. Angie relaxes on the comfy chair as Stephanie goes back upstairs to finish making cookies and to check on Denise. Before leaving she teases, "Don't pass out." It was only six months earlier at the Canada Day barbeque she thought she could beat Michelle at a shot drinking game and had her belligerent former self carried to the basement couch on which she now sits upon. Denise comes downstairs following her mom, who sets the cookies down, and Denise clearly already got into the brownies or chocolate cake as the edges of her tiny mouth are stained. Denise refuses to let Angie wipe her mouth clean and runs back upstairs. Not long after, there's a soft knock on the back door. Karen has arrived and greets Angie with a smile, unable to hug as she has spent her time baking fried bread and puts it on the table.

"I'm going back to Terrace tonight, after the dinner is over. My aunt wants me close by. She fears old dramas might erupt if I stay at home." Karen says.

Earlier, Angie looked up severe depression online and learned anti-depressants isn't an instant cure. It actually takes a few weeks before the pills are effective. It relieves her to hear there's family looking out for her during this brief period. Karen takes off her coat and puts it on the homemade rack consisting of nails in the dry wall. She fishes for something in her coat pocket and then walks solemnly to the head of the table. On the table is a picture of Walt sitting at the Chinese food place in Terrace, a picture Angie took the year before that was rediscovered by his parents. Walt smiles happily at the camera with his hands on the table clasped like a news anchor on the television. Karen puts a small present next to the photo before quietly walking upstairs.

Angie goes outside for air. When she used to smoke she would sneak out the back door, hoping nobody would bug or pester her to kick the habit. She admires the numerous external Christmas lights of the houses up and down the street. Another car pulls into the driveway and parks next to Karen's car, or the car her aunt let her borrow. Walt's grandmother happily smiles and waves as she hops out of the van. Walt's cousin Eric hurries to hold his grandmother's arm as they walk toward the back door. Eric's mom has a large bowl full of hot spaghetti. "No smoking," his grandmother says as she walks in the house.

"Yeah, no smoking," Eric jokingly repeats before they close the door.

Angie remembers the present she bought Eric, and she makes a note to give it to him at the dinner table later. She walks around the freshly shoveled backyard, admiring the sorted wood in the shed as she notes the slow-burning last-all-night wood is on the left side and the fast-burning wood on the right side. Angie realizes her woodshed at the house is just a jumbled pile of wood lazily tossed in all together with no order. Every time Angie comes out here she keeps looking up at his bedroom window. Coming to this house always hurts. Either it's the sight of the pitch-black room that has the window blinds closed shut, or it's when she goes to the bathroom and the steel padlock on the door catches her eye. She remembers to breathe and stave off the sick feeling she has been getting here and there—just a punch in the gut that makes her want to vomit. The only time she ever felt that was at graduation when she was asked to make a speech, standing in front of several hundred bored people wanting her to get it over with so they could all go to their respective grad parties and dinners. She thinks maybe she should follow Karen's lead, go see a doctor and make sure she's not ruining her health or causing probable ulcers. Before going in, Angie checks the snow. It is moist and heavy, it's nearly ready to bring Denise out so they can make a baby snowman.

One by one people pull into the driveway and arrive for the dinner. The family originally wanted to host a bigger dinner, a non-feast feast at the community hall, but it was booked in advance by the various village sporting organizations that are hosting family games nights all week long leading up to the New Year's dance. Walt's dad opens the dinner with a prayer, and Stephanie unwraps all the food. Everyone queues up in order just as Stephanie planned and everyone gets in line to make their way around the pool table picking up their favorite foods. Walt's mom goes first—she's making his plate. And when she is done she walks to the stove and everyone watches her throw it in the fire for her son. After that, everyone is free to pick and grab what they want to eat.

Angie smirks to herself thinking Walt's *Duh-uhs* (cheeks) would be so red from all the stories told tonight. Stories that weren't exactly appropriate to tell at his Memorial last month, not mean-spirited tales, just loving recollections they had of him when he was still alive. His grandmother set the tone when she recounted everyone driving back south from the north, buckets full of picked blueberries in the back of the family truck. His grandfather loved to spoil Walt and treated him as much as he could, and would give infant Walt berries when he'd reach for them. Not long after passing Mezia-din Junction they all noticed the smell, opening the windows didn't help, and Walt's uncle stopped the truck to change his diaper. His grandmother laughed when she forced his grand-father to do the honors. She remembers him going to the back tailgate, cloth diapers in hand. Through the mirror she saw her husband run into the bush gagging at the unholy mess he had made. He still spoiled all his grandkids, but knew not to go overboard like that again. Unknown to Walt, his first nickname was Blue.

The dinner slowly comes to a close and everyone sits there full from eating everything. Denise is wired from the chocolates and goodies people have been giving her. "Don't puke in your mom's ear like Walt did to mine," Eric's mom jokes, remembering the time she babysat Walt when he was a little kid; he was fed too much fast food in Terrace and got sick in his aunt's ear on the way home.

"Man, he had a story for every orifice," Michelle jokes.

Peter reaches into his art bag and pulls out two framed pieces he had made for Walt's parents and for Angie. When Walt and Peter were little punk kids nearly entering high school, they started a comic series about the rez. Comics about bingo, comics about all the stray dogs, and comics about bologna making people horny. The framed pieces are passed around the tables, and everyone laughs at the crude humor. The origin story of Bologna Man who flies around smacking people or animals in the head with bologna putting a stop to conflict. In one series, Bologna Man comes across a couple fighting outside the village hall, smack, the next frame there's a picture of a van making rocking gestures and vibrations. Just silly cartoons the two thought were hilarious at the time.

Angie has the realization, "Oh my god. Doug. That's you! You're Bologna Man."

Doug tries to deny it, and his face gets red at being teased. Walt's dad goes to the garage freezer and comes back with an arm-sized bulk tube of bologna, Gilbert says, "Hold it up heroically." It's not long before people take his picture, chest outstretched, holding the frozen bologna above his head.

"Once this gets on the internet it's there forever, Doug," Michelle teases.

This was a good night, a happy night, and Angie is sure Walt enjoyed it too. The people that did bring presents for Walt approach the hot burning stove, and when they open it there's no sign of the food given earlier. Each person quietly wishes Walt a happy Christmas, tries to put into words how much they miss him, and give him a present. This isn't a normal tradition for the dead, but a few people wanted to do this as they deal with the loss. Eric thanks Angie for the video game she gifted him for Christmas and promises to tell her how far he gets when he plays it. Karen tells everyone she won't be a stranger when she gets back next spring after school ends. Slowly, people announce they are leaving to go home, or stop and watch the games up at the gym. It's just Walt's family now sitting at the table, occasionally laughing at the stories, or taking a peek at Doug's Bologna Man pose. Gilbert says, "Denise, take Aunty Angie upstairs and show her your Christmas present."

Angie, now curious, wonders what else the little girl got for Christmas. Denise takes Angie's hand and tries running upstairs, Angie's stride is out of sync with Denise's and it's a clumsy go of it. Denise refuses the offer to be carried up the stairs. Angie focuses on making sure her little cousin doesn't go falling down the stairs, guiding her and supporting her as she climbs. "Where are you going? That door is locked." It's then Angie notices the change. The door has the padlock removed, and only empty screw holes remain. There's a new engraved wooden plaque on the door, just under where it says, "Walt," there's a sign that reads, "Denise Joanna." DJ pushes the door open, stands on a stair stool, and reaches up to turn on the lights. The room has been painted with childlike replicas of the surrounding mountains: Red Rose Mountain, Roche De Bull, Patty Mountain, and Gitsegukla Mountain. On the other side of the wall is Andamal Mountain and even the Seven Sisters range. Angie wonders who did all this, but Denise doesn't know, she only woke up and was shown the room after Christmas breakfast. On one half, the sky is bright blue, on the other half big, yellow, nighttime stars contrast with a dark purple sky. Angie looks at the detail of the painting, she sees First Nations crests of the Grouse and Frog Clan at the closet door, of her grandparents' houses. Lined up along the wall are framed photos of Walt with Denise during the three years they had together. A shelf has all the stuffed toys he gave her when he would come back from school or trips abroad. There's a little child's princess bed with pink blankets and pillows. Denise shows Angie everything that she can: all the toys she got for Christmas, the educational books on the shelf, and Walt's favorite books still on the upper part of the shelf. Angie has one of her first maternal thoughts: that if she ever had a baby of her own she would want the room to be as amazing as Denise's new room.

Stephanie and Angie sit at the kitchen table still trying to digest the food. "It was my dad, me, and Peter who did the painting. While Denise went to visit her great grandmother and aunts. Dad paid the carver in Hagwilget to do a new sign plaque for her door, like he did the one for me and Walt when we moved into this house." Angie can't get used to the sight of the door being open or the change of color from drab white-painted walls to the colorful mosaic Denise will now call home. "You were right. We all felt the same way too. Coming home from work or even going to the kitchen, the padlock was a knife stabbing us with hurt every time we'd see it. We'd cry when Denise wanted to go in there to visit her *Bii'*. At first, we didn't want to touch the room, but then we couldn't leave it alone either. So we thought, let's make Denise an amazing bedroom now that she's getting older and try pack it full of things so she never forgets her *Bii'*." It took some time before Angie caught on that *Bii'* means uncle. "Before you go home, this is for you." Stephanie gives Angie a plastic baggy. She looks at it and smiles, it's a handful of glow-in-the-dark star stickers for the ceiling. "We didn't want to leave you out, we'd never leave you out, so go crazy and put some stickers up in her room." Angie does, trying to be random and spontaneous, but also intently putting up real constellations to instill a curiosity in astronomy. Her finishing touch is a replica of the constellation Walt put in Angie's bedroom. A little cat-shaped head with a smiley face in the corner of the room above the bed.

* * *

Angie's last week in the village is a mixture of sleeping in until 11am some mornings or getting up bright and early. She often would go play with Denise and take her sliding at the dam and even doing some skating at the rink in Terrace. As much as she tried to she couldn't extend her stay in the village by keeping busy or lounging around watching movies with Michelle and Peter at the gas station. Time was running out, and school in Prince George was waiting for her after the start of the New Year. Getting a head start, she already packed her suitcases, and loaded up the still-sealed textbooks she had bought in the back of her SUV. She'd rather do this days in advance than at the last minute and forget anything. This would leave her plenty of time to enjoy being with her friends and family before making the five-hour drive east. Today is the last day of the year, and tonight there will be a fireworks show hosted by the local volunteer firemen and a dry dance for everyone at the gym. Even though there is a planned fireworks display, Walt's father dragged his daughter Stephanie along to pick up fireworks in Kitwanga, a tradition they have kept since childhood. Angie hasn't decided what her plans are for the evening. She'll be with her mom and Walt's family enjoying both fireworks shows, but she's had a few offers to leave the village for New Year's dances outside the village where alcohol will be permitted.

When she approaches the house, it strikes Angie that it's unusually quiet—she's always been used to Walt's grandmother hosting many guests when visiting in the past. Upon entering, she sees Eric stirring his tea, and he quickly informs Angie how far he got in the game and how much fun it is. He thanks Angie again for the Christmas present received. She sits down at the table and is served a hot bowl of moose soup. Angie crunches up crackers to put on top of it and makes a few cracker and butter sandwiches. She learns everyone went up the back roads to go do some hunting for rabbit or moose, which is why the house feels so quiet, and they will be back before it gets dark. The soup has generous chunks of potatoes, celery, onions, noodles, and meat—some still on the bone. When she finishes eating she washes her bowl and spoon in the sink before joining Walt's grandmother on the couch. She always liked his grandmother, always so welcoming and hospitable. She wasn't as goofy as Michelle's grandmother, but still a sweet old lady. Angie only recently learned her late grandmother and Walt's grandmother were best friends way back in the day. "Sometimes I have to catch myself and not call you Shirley, since you look just like her, if only I was young again too." She laughs as she goes to the shelf in the corner of the room. Walt's grandmother hands Angie an envelope explaining, "My daughter told me you started a book, a capturing of his life. That's a good thing, remembering those we lost. Yesterday I went through my albums and picked these out for you." Angie opens the envelope and recognizes some of the pictures from when the two looked through the albums before the Memorial service. One picture at the end stands out—she never saw that photo before.

His grandmother speaks of her illness she fought and beat several years ago, an illness that has taken a lot of the community's elders: cancer. She talks of the long treatment plan she had to endure, recalling being so sick, so tired, and so scared. Everyone rallied around her as she beat the cancer. The whole family rented a restaurant in Hazelton and they had a big celebration when she came back from Vancouver. It was February when the doctor delivered the bad news that the cancer had returned. She speaks of feeling terrified thinking it was out to get her, and her time with everyone she loved so limited. Walt's aunts went to Vancouver for the next round of treatments, but the tests and progress reports weren't promising. Angie remembers stopping by after school and finding Walt and Stephanie in the basement crying during that first month. They had spent their childhoods being raised by their grandmother, coming down to eat lunch when they were still in elementary school or coming after school to help do chores. It's not so different from how Angie has come to be familiar with Walt's parents in the past few years. Their home is a safe little space she can visit when she needs to. Walt used to talk about that month, of it being so sad to come to this house and find it empty, and how everything seemed wrong that his

Geech wasn't home. After school had ended everyone packed up to go to Vancouver. The general feeling was that this was near the end. "I wanted to go for a walk that morning with my two oldest grand kids. Stephanie and Walt took me to Stanley Park, and we made it to the sea wall. I remember both of them so clearly in my mind, crying when we stopped at the bench. They thought I had wanted to take them out there and give them the bad news that I was dying. I didn't know their mom had taken this picture until a few months later." Walt's grandmother asks to look at the picture after telling her story. The ocean is a hazy blue, the sky is blue with some light clouds, and sitting on the bench on both sides of her are Walt and Stephanie. "Time is precious, you never know how long you have with the ones you love, and just like that they can be gone. You know that, I know that. It catches up with all of us eventually, there's no outrunning it. Enjoy life. Enjoy the ones you love. And don't sit there when you're too weak and frail, regretting you didn't do something you wanted to do out in the world when it's too late. That's what I told my two grandkids on the bench, in this picture." She broke the happy news to them that she was going to live, and they'd all come home again and things would go back to normal. "He will always be right there with you, Angie. It hurts right now, I can see it in your eyes, and I felt the same when my *Ye'eh* left us. It is okay to feel this pain. Don't feel ashamed when you miss him so much or feel like crying. Just remember you are alive, he wants you to live and be happy. Even though he's not here with us in body, Walt will always be with us in our hearts."

It is freezing as the soon-to-be-January winds blow against

everyone standing in the near dark. They are all on the hill, looking down at the firemen as they prepare for their show. Everyone who hasn't left the village to go to other dances soon makes their way to the Band Office and Health Center parking lots. People are keeping an eye on the clock, waiting for the countdown. Angie stands with Michelle, both of them holding Denise's hands, and they show her where to look when the time comes. Stephanie and her parents keep warm in the truck, listening to rock music. "There's Bologna Man, getting ready to light them off." Michelle laughs as she points out Doug who recently joined the firefighters. Without warning, people start counting down, voices in unison starting from "10." Just as they reach "1" the village fire hall siren goes off, and dogs start howling in response. The popping of fireworks has started all around the village. Michelle and Angie look around them as some families opt to do their own fireworks displays in their yards. The sound of celebratory shotguns being fired can be heard higher up in the village. The firemen start igniting their fireworks, and the New Year has begun.

People can be heard yelling, "Happy New Year!"

As they stand there in the cold, watching the multicolored explosions in the sky, Angie silently cries, not sobbing, just tears. This is the first year without Walt in it. After it is over she rides with his parents up to their house for the second show. Michelle, Stephanie, and Walt's dad make an effort to synchronize lighting the fireworks so a bunch go off at the same time. It's not long before a crowd forms at the driveway, watching several hundred dollars explode above. Denise loves it, as she is packed by her grandmother, and reaches to the sky. Even Angie got in on the action and lit the last batch of fireworks, she ran away before they went off, and watched at a safe distance. Afterwards everyone went in the basement to warm up, eat a platter of cheese and crackers Stephanie prepared, and then put Denise to sleep. Friends were catching up with each other, talking about their imminent plans, and hugging or shaking hands wishing each other a better New Year.

She wakes up feeling neither sick, nor hung over, since she had the sense to avoid drinking last night. The house is quiet, her mom's door is closed, and she can hear her snoring, and in the guest room Michelle is sprawled out on the bed. Angie chose to stay in the village. Michelle and Angie first went to the dry dance and had some fun on the floor before stopping at Peter's for a quiet get together. Angie helped Michelle stagger to her home at 3 in the morning, and that was how the New Year started. She makes the largest batch of pancakes, bacon, sausages, hash browns, and scrambled eggs that she can. Eventually the other two wake up sick, grateful for some food, jealous of Angie who doesn't have a pounding headache. Soon after, Michelle goes home to probably be scolded by her grandmother, but Angie did her a favor and let her *Jiits* know that she was okay the night before, and that Angie would look after her.

The sky is clear when she steps out the front door to take an overdue walk. A few houses down she can see the smoky remnants of a family's Christmas tree that was set ablaze the night before. The ground is cold; she doesn't really think he's in the ground as she sits talking to him. Angie thinks he's out there somewhere instead, she can feel it. Nobody else is in the graveyard visiting departed loved ones. Angie tells Walt about things that have changed in the two months since he died. How big Denise is getting and how beautiful her room is. That both his parents are okay, and his *Geech* is okay. She asks him to watch over Karen. "I don't know what you were thinking, but Sam could have been an awesome girlfriend for you, so *Gooch*." None of this she says out loud. Angie always found it hokey to do teary-eyed graveside monologues like they do in the movies. These are just little thoughts Angie says in her head. She gets up, brushing the snow off her pants and coat, leaves a simple bouquet of flowers, and walks back to her house.

Two days later there are no dramatic teary-eyed good-byes. No one chasing her in slow motion as she turns off the bumpy, sanded reserve road and onto Highway 16 eastbound. The roads are mostly clear, with some patches of compact snow, and no dangerous January black ice conditions. It will stay this way until five or six, and her dad told her not to drive after dark if she can help it. Angie stops in Hazelton to pick up a light stock of sandwiches, chips, and water if she ever found herself stranded waiting for roadside help. Already she misses home, and she's only been gone for twenty minutes. On the two-lane section outside of Hazelton she lets the more impatient drivers pass her. She wants to keep a respectable pace until she gets to Prince George. Forty minutes later, she is now at the edge of Smithers. This is it, she's officially out of Gitksan territory, but technically the large village named

Witset is the boundary between Gitksan and Wetsuweten territories. For her, anything east of Smithers she doesn't consider *home*. Soon, the mountains and hill sides become alien. The trees feel darker and less inviting. The towns she'll be driving through are anonymous houses and buildings filled with strangers. She wonders if people feel the same way when they drive through Gitsegukla, that it's just this small little curiosity on the way to Terrace or Prince Rupert. They don't have an appreciation for people living in such a community, its traditions or its history.

It's an intentionally quiet drive, the only sound being the gravel kicking up against the vehicle exterior from the highway department's sanding treatment. There was a time Doug and Angie's friend, Crystal, from Kispiox, would carpool together when they returned to school in Prince George. They already arranged travel plans, so it's her going solo this time, and she misses the company. Angie has never liked the drive to Prince George from Gitsegukla, and she realizes why now: the maintained evergreens are tall and haunting, yet feel empty and barren. She wants to get the drive over with already, past the low hills, the frozen lakes, and too-peaceful fields. Angie isn't far from a First Nations-run gas bar outside Fort Frasier. She wonders if that place has a girl like Michelle working there? Angie wants her friend to join her at college already, but Michelle is on a waiting list for funding. Angie now approaches a steep and curved hill that still gives her nightmares. The first time she descended it, it felt like she would go careening off the edge to her doom below. This time it's a slow climb up the hill where the roads get thankfully more straight and easier to navigate. It's just then it happens—for a moment she thought it was in her head, but she knows it's real. Looking down slightly to her left shoulder, and then in the rear-view mirror, she sees nothing, but feels the sensation of her seatbelt being tugged to get her attention. It tightens the same way it would if she suddenly slammed her brakes when confronted with a yellow light in Prince George. Angie takes another look in the rear-view mirror—nobody is back there, and she physically checks to be sure. This leaves her unsettled and scared. Angie slows her car down further. Going from 85 kilometers down to 50, and slower as she decides to pull over and redo her seatbelt at the top of the hill where the semi-trucks normally pull over to do their brake checks. After the truck reaches the top of the hill she sees them. Angie stops and pulls off the road, looking at them: two big moose with one baby moose following. They are right in the middle of the eastbound lane. Angie has a flashback to seeing Walt's dad's car crumpled when he hit a moose near Seeley Lake several years ago. Gilbert was lucky to have escaped that accident without serious injury. Angie realizes if she was going at her previous speed and had crossed the crest of the hill it would have been bad. Angie would have either rammed right into them or tried going off the road, swerving to avoid them and maybe even rolling into the ditch until she hit the trees. After fishing the phone out of the glove box, she snaps a picture of the family of moose, then honks her horn, prompting them to slowly lumber off the road into the bush. Hands shaking at the close call, Angie refits her seatbelt, puts the car back into drive, and resumes her trip. The rest of the way is uneventful except for some obnoxious tailgaters outside Vanderhoof.

When Angie hauls her belongings to her dorm room, she meets her roommates from the previous year; they are happy to see her again. Both offer their condolences, giving hugs, and then asking to go out for dinner. The dorm room is chilly—she turns up the electric heat, missing the wood stove at home, and then makes the bed. Right now, she would call Toronto letting Walt know she made it there safely. Angie calls her mom and texts Michelle, letting them know she made it there in one piece. Angie makes a point of deciding that she won't regress like in November. She will not sit on the bed sad and depressed. Instead, she puts her things away and decides to take up her friends on their offer of pizza and wings. Angie is excited to finally get back to school after the long time off; a part of her misses home, but she can easily go back every couple of weekends. Her mom promised to visit, too, once in a while. Before forgetting, she opens up the folio and takes out the picture, the photo her dad gave her two months before. Two cousins on their way to the aquarium to see the whales. Two cousins who would become best friends. A slight moment of sadness passes, but is replaced with gratitude. A feeling of calm, the twisted knot in her stomach not there anymore. He was doing what he always did, looking out for her when she needed it. Walt saved her one more time, and one day she will thank him when they meet again. Angie knows this now.

Headstone and Fence

Sitting there on the nice cool rocks, the feeling of sunburn creeps up on her. She had the sense to bring sun screen, so it's just the heat of late August bearing down. Not far off down the beach she sees two people fishing with poles, instead of using nets like other people who set them across the river. The river looks so green, no longer brown and muddy like it was when it flooded in the spring. The Skeena River is flowing at its regular pace, and the accompanying breeze is pleasant. She has no more time to fool around, she needs to get back. Slapping another mosquito, Angie wishes it was winter again. While many people in Gitsegukla enjoy the summer lifestyle of soccer tournaments, barbeques, and late-night parties with bonfires, Angie is the only one who enjoys the snow. Angie pines for the freezing cold, the slippery roads, and complete lack of mosquitos. She walks up the hill, past the "Welcome to Gitsegukla" sign, and crosses the long bridge back into the village. Angie is mindful of her surroundings, since there were reports of black bears a few days earlier. Standing in the middle of the bridge, she stops and takes a panoramic shot of the nearby mountains, a few still have white snow on their peaks. The village feels alive when she passes under the overpass. Out there, little kids can be heard playing tag, soccer, or riding their bikes. A few cars are cruising around with music blaring out the windows. She sees her mom's car parked at the band office and tries waving at her when she passes by as she goes to the house. The house is still warm when Angie enters, and she wishes they had air conditioning. She takes a quick shower and changes into more appropriate clothing.

Angie crosses the street to visit her neighbors. They're not in the house, she knows that as she can hear them behind the house laughing and talking. A huge chunk of the backyard has waist-high grass needing to be cut, but it's been ages since anyone with a scythe chopped it all down. The only maintained parts of Michelle's backyard are the spaces around the wood shed and the smoke house, the *Wilp Se'huun*.

Michelle says, "Look at miss fancy pants coming up here in her dress."

Michelle laughs, saying something in Gitksan to her grandmother.

Her grandmother asks, "Is it time?"

Angie answers indicating people are still getting ready. Michelle's grandmother goes inside the smoke house, opening the door and letting out a puff of blue smoke. She returns, handing Angie a tiny sliver of smoked salmon that was hanging inside.

Angie gives it a taste, she says, "Still soft, the salt feels just right, but needs more time." Michelle's grandmother agrees, happy Angie is learning quickly how to make her own *Hooxsw*.

Michelle's grandmother says, "You should leave now, don't want to ruin your dress with the smell of smoke or the fish."

Angie reminds them of the time, saying, "My mom hasn't

wrapped up work just yet. I'm going back to check the cooking. I'll pick you guys up in an hour."

Unlike Michelle's backyard, Walt's father keeps up maintaining the grass around his house, excluding the brush and trees at the edge of the property. Angie stands there admiring the freshly cut lawn, the little path of stepping stones that runs alongside the driveway, and a picnic table recently acquired. Denise, now four years old, is talking with her mom about cookies and soup, wearing a bright blue dress nearly matching the one Angie is wearing. Nobody parks in the driveway when they pull up to the house. It's a moderate gathering of twenty to thirty people, friends of the family and relatives. This is a day that has been planned for several months now, and the pieces have fallen into place. Walt's mother addresses everyone standing in the yard. Nadine thanks them for taking the time to come out this afternoon. She reminds everyone that if they're hot or thirsty drinks are by the picnic table. This isn't a family picnic and barbeque, though it feels like it as people talk amongst themselves, catching up with friends or relatives. Angie listens to Michelle talk about how she almost sliced open her thumb cutting salmon strips, showing her the little cut. Angie points to the pair across the field.

"Look, they remember each other." Angie says, she stares at a young three-and-a-half-year-old boy with dark hair playing catch with Denise, she continues, "I feel so old, they're still little babies."

Angie's dad comes up from behind the two, he says, "You feel old, what does that say about me?"

Angie hugs her dad, happy to see him. Angie sees her stepmom eating *Is*, Indian ice cream, for the first time with Walt's mom.

Angie says, "She's never had foamy soap berries before, I wonder if she'll like them."

The three watch curiously, then chuckle when she makes a weird face at the unique flavor. Walt's mom takes the bowl of foamy pink cream from Angie's stepmom and offers her fried bread instead. Michelle slaps a mosquito on her arm, looking at the crushed, bloody spot before wiping it away on her pants. "It would be nice if this village got treated for mosquitos like Hazelton and Terrace."

Angie checks her watch and it is nearly two in the afternoon. The family decides to let people enjoy the gathering before officially beginning the event. People hush down in silence as both of Walt's parents stand in front of their house entrance. Standing beside them is his sister Stephanie, little Denise, and his grandmother. Speaking loudly so everyone can hear, Walt's mother explains how things will happen now that everyone is here, and they're ready to begin, "Angie, we call upon you to do this task for us. You are like a daughter to us, and he thought of you as a kid sister to look after. It only feels right that you be the one to do this." Angie walks to the two parents and hugs them. She still feels odd with everyone watching her, it's not her way to be the center of attention. The two parents hand Angie a cloth and a bowl of water. Angie takes them and walks to the side of the house where it is located. Bending down on one knee, she ignores the pesky mosquitos, but has a wary eye on a bee not far away, and focuses on her task. Angie has been entrusted with washing the headstone, his headstone that was ordered and delivered that very week, a headstone that will be taken down to Walt's grave where it will rest. She feels a sense of duty as she washes the cool marble stone with the cloth. A thin layer of dust from village traffic settled on it after being exposed to the elements for just a day. Angie admires the work put into the stone, the epitaph, and looking at the dates. It has been nine months since his passing. It feels like so much has happened since then, but she still misses her cousin dearly. After washing the headstone Angie gets up, exchanges the water and cloth for a dry towel, then gently dries the headstone before returning to Michelle and her mother's side. The parents thank Angie for everything she has done.

Next, the family calls up Peter's father, a spiritual leader in the community, to bless the headstone. Everyone is solemn and quiet as he speaks the Gitksan prayer. Praying for the family to heal, to bless the headstone, and wishing Walt a safe journey to the other side. When he is done he shakes the family's hand and returns to the crowd. Everyone resumes briefly chatting with another while admiring the headstone in its temporary resting space. Before the next part begins the family gestures for pictures to be taken. The first group is of Walt's parents, sister, and niece standing in front of the headstone—no smiles, just a quiet respectful picture. Angie and her half-brother, Morgan, stand next to the headstone, and Denise not wanting to be left out, stands next to her cousins. Walt's grandmother, aunts, and uncles then take their picture.

Angie stands next to her dad, listening to him talk with his friends about the headstone, and its cost. If Walt had a Gitksan name or a Chief's name when he died whoever took his name at the Funeral Feast would be obligated to buy the headstone and fence, as that is the custom in Gitksan culture. When a person has done that task, they have solidified their claim on the name they inherited and can proudly use the name in the Feast Hall without shame or doubt. But, Walt didn't have a Gitksan name when he suddenly passed away. Instead, the family has taken on the financial responsibility of paying for the headstone and fence, and everyone has helped as much as they can in this special case.

In the olden days Gitsegukla village was still small and most of the population lived on the other side of the highway. Transporting the headstone to the graveyard would be done with a wagon, pulled by a rope or the handle. As time passed, the people moved higher up the hill and the community got bigger; the headstone pulling ceremony needed to adapt to the times. The headstone has carefully been moved to the back of the truck, driven by Walt's godfather just as he drove the casket the year before. Doug and Peter sit in the back of the truck, ensuring the headstone doesn't move around as they make the long trip to the graveyard, especially when they hit any potholes or bumps along the way, continuing their duties as the pallbearers. Walt's father has finished tying a rope to the front bumper of the truck, a modern take on the headstone pulling where instead of a wagon they will faux pull the truck. Arrangements were made in advance so nobody would be surprised when the names were announced, and people from the father's clan are invited to take part when called upon. Chiefs from Gilbert's clan are called up to the front of the group, members of *Ganada*, the Frog Clan. They stand in front of the truck and then pick up the rope that was tied to the bumper. This is a light affair, not so serious or solemn, and pictures are taken. The walk to the graveyard will now begin.

Angie walks with her brother and Denise, and both want to hold her hand as they follow the truck. They can keep up because the pace is slow and steady. Walt's parents are ahead of her and they are talking about the evenings plans, ensuring they haven't forgotten anything. The group of people walking, sweating in the hot summer sun, has now grown to over forty in attendance. Karen joins after arriving late from her summer job. Michelle is at the back of the group, driving her grandmother in their truck, they were entrusted with bringing essential items needed when they arrive at the graveyard. At various points during the slow walk down the hill, the people holding the rope change and are replaced by other Frog Clan members, like a relay. New Chiefs from the father's clan take the rope, to do their part of the ceremony. One day, Angie will do this. She just recently learned she will have a name of her own, a true Gitksan name. With that, comes the responsibilities and duties expected of such a title, even though it's a smaller name. She will need to participate in the Feast hall as she does. She will need to sharpen up on her Gitksan language skills and understanding of the words. She's well on her way in learning how to prepare traditional foods and meals from her elders. Michelle has been dragging her up to the gym, so she's been learning traditional dances and Gitksan songs of her clan.

In this slow walk, Angie recalls the feverish pleading she did that cold day in November, childishly begging her cousin to wake up from death; that slight bout of mania that was consuming her as she tried cheating the grief she was going through. Angie still misses her cousin—she habitually wants to call him on the phone, and is sad when she wakes up from dreams in which he visited her. Nine months is not enough time for the pain to completely fade away. Angie got so mad when some guy at college callously told her to get over it and be happy already. You can't rush grief, and special people in life can't be replaced. Angie smiles instead as she thinks pleasant thoughts and memories of him. She's hopeful the two little ones holding her hands will become just as good friends, and will have the special relationship she once had with Walt, one day. Angie looks back at a now taller Eric who is following in Walt's footsteps, an avid gamer who also wants to get into computer programing and video game making. Angie has been encouraging him as much as she can. Not just by buying him video games, but by providing beginner's programming and computer science books and tutoring him with the knowledge she's picked up. Angie looks around at everyone in the group now walking past her house. Everyone here remembers him, and they miss him too. They honor him by being here today and observe one of the final acts of putting him to rest.

The headstone now rests by his grave, the fence neatly installed. It stands there next to his grandfather's plot. Tears are shed as people look on at the stone. They cry at how unfair it was to lose him so young. Angie takes a final look at the headstone before she returns to the group that has gathered around Michelle's truck. Walt's mother and grandmother prepared a special treat for everyone. They have cooked several pots of mashed potatoes and salt fish, *Hashbadinner*. Also, there are platters of fried salmon that were cooked over an open flame, searing the skin and cooking the meat. It is crunchy when bitten into, cooked similarly to how campers make toast on an open fire. Everyone is served some food and drink, and near the end of the ceremony Walt's parents announce the time. A last Feast is to be hosted at the hall that very evening, a Feast the family has been preparing for the past week, ensuring there's enough fruit, enough bread, and soda. They were organizing Grouse Clan members in cooking delicious soups. The Feast will not be like the Funeral Feast, there will be no giving of the *Hawal*. Instead, it will be the family publicly thanking everyone who helped with the moving of the headstone. Later that evening, Angie will be given five dollars for washing the headstone, and Peter's dad will be given five dollars for blessing the headstone. The Chiefs from the Frog Clan who helped "pull" the headstone will receive five dollars as well. It will be a good Feast, people will get full, stories of Walt will be told, and everyone can take a step forward after this loss and find their way.

"Look at miss fancy pants wearing her dirty sweatpants and sweatshirt to my smoke house," Michelle mocks as Angie makes her way across the street the day after. The two walk around to the back smoke house, each taking a seat and dressing freshly caught salmon delivered by Walt's father. They slowly cut thin strips of salmon, lightly salting them before setting them aside. They will soon be left to hang in the smoke house, developing their unique flavor and texture. Angie has a serene smile on her face as Michelle tells stories about the weird customers she puts up with at her new summer job managing the grocery store in Hazelton. Michelle knows her story isn't that entertaining and asks Angie what's the deal with her smile. "Did you *Un* someone and not tell me? Are you *Ubin* now? Was it Peter? Did Peter get you pregnant?" Michelle laughs.

It was a hot summer day, the last day of August. It might have been September, she didn't know. There she was walking on this weird dirt road she never saw before. It took her a while to get her bearings, but she could see Red Rose Mountain in the east. In the south, a pale crescent moon was hanging low near Gitsegukla Mountain. She was close to home, her internal compass was telling her, maybe above the village on the old logging road. Angie was thankful the mosquitos were ignoring her. She arrived at a bend in the road—the logging road would turn and twist down a sharp ravine. Near the bend was a clearing, and Angie could make out the familiar signs that this clearing was used for parking. Rather than go further down the logging road she stared at a faint path made by people who had waded through tall, uncut grass, a worn trail made by many footprints. Angie wasn't ready for a hike; she had no walking stick or a backpack, and she knew better than to just go off into the bush without telling anyone. Angie had seen too many stories on the evening news of lost hikers needing rescuing. But she had felt something pulling her to take a few steps, to see what was out there on the forgotten trail. The forest canopy quickly made the air cool and pleasant. The moss was soft under her shoes. Birds were chirping randomly in the forest, and the entire situation too much like a fairy tale. The trees felt ancient and seemed to get bigger the farther she hiked. The trail rose and dipped eastward, the sound of a creek flowing getting louder, and soon Angie found herself at the water's edge.

A twig snaps and Angie turns around, hearing a voice, "Little Bear." Angie sees him wearing a backpack and holding a walking stick. Walt smiles as he hugs Angie. The sensation of her throat trying to swallow lumps keeps her from speaking or making any noise, and she feels only happiness and relief.

When Walt lets go Angie grabs his hands, Angie begs, "Come, come with me, we can go back to the village."

Walt's smile fades away, he stands there staring at Angie. She asks, "Where are you going?"

Walt answers, "Up the mountain. They're ahead of me."

Angie asks, "Can I come too?"

He smiles and shakes his head, no. Angie realizes this is a dream, or is it really a dream but something more? Angie hugs Walt, not wanting to let go, not wanting to wake up.

"Timber!" a soft voice bellows from the other side of the creek.

A tree falls with a thick thud, creating a makeshift bridge

across the water. Angie stares confused as the familiar man emerges from the brush, her old basketball coach? "The Bear" waves and walks away on the trail.

"He's always been there for me. Both of them have." Says Walt.

Angie sees an older man she never met, a man she only saw in photo albums, a man she only knew as his *Ye'eh*. He smiles and continues up the path, following the coach. It's just the two of them again, standing at the creek. "I know you have to go now and head up the mountain, Walt, and that I can't follow. There are all these things I want to tell you, but maybe I don't have to. I don't think I've ever said it, not without it being weird. You are my favorite person in the world. I love you, I miss you every day. Thank you for all the times you looked out for me. Don't be a stranger, okay?" Walt smiles, gives her another big hug, and then steps back. Angie watches him apprehensively cross the tree that was turned into a bridge, using the walking stick to keep from falling. Walt turns back to see her, waves, and smiles as he walks on a path heading up the mountain.

"I had a dream last night. It was a beautiful dream. I want to tell everybody what I saw." Angie says, she slices another thin strip off her salmon. She puts it on the pile that is ready to be hung in the smoke house. In a few months, they will be enjoying the *Hooxsw* she has made. In a few months, they will share the dream too.